Dark Red
The Beginning of the End

By Walter Masterson

www.wmasterson.com
Cover design by Janet Howard-Fatta
www.howardstudios.com

Printed in the United States of America
First Printing: November 2011
3rd Edition – April 2014
ISBN: 1467969087
ISBN-13: 978-1467969086

DEDICATION

This book is dedicated to Karen who has taught me with both her words and deeds to move forward with my dreams, and past my reservations. She was instrumental in helping me transition from a career in the financial industry to being a therapist. The word "can't" is not part of her vocabulary, and she has inspired me to remove it from mine.

Table of Contents

Acknowledgments

This book would have been still-born, but for my friend Songhui. As I wrote each new chapter, my absorption with the book's story grew, and eventually became an obsession. I no longer had the perspective to evaluate how it was progressing, whether it made sense to anyone but me, or had merit of any kind. After completing half a dozen chapters my uncertainty became so acute that I stopped writing. The book was dead.

During a chance conversation with Songhui I mentioned the abandoned work; she asked to read what I'd done. She called me two days later, full of excitement for the story and hot to see where I was going with it. She devoured each additional chapter I produced, until the book was finished. Her enthusiasm for the work never flagged and by itself nurtured me through the process. Without her Dark Red would not have happened.

Then there is Jackie, a good friend and fellow sailor, who looks after me when I go off half-cocked. She has been a continuous source of strength and guidance in the second most difficult part of being an author - getting published. I am blessed to have the support of these extraordinary friends.

Prologue

"It is only in and through people, inwardly developed men and women, that God can exist and act in the world of man on earth. Bluntly speaking, the proof for the existence of God is the existence of people who are inhabited by and who manifest God... God needs not just man, but awakened man, in order to act as God in the human world. Without this conscious energy on the earth it may not be possible for divine justice, mercy, or compassion to enter the lives of human beings."

From "What is God" by Jacob Needleman

Afghanistan

IN A SMALL AFGHAN VILLAGE forty kilometers east of the Pakistani tribal areas, a group of men stood in a semi-circle around the village elder. The old man said nothing for several moments. He stared down at the few scorched artifacts that remained of his sons and their possessions taken from the site where they had been murdered. It was impossible to tell what was going through his mind. Finally he spoke.

"Bring the boy to me."

After a few moments a young man was brought before him. He was a boy of perhaps twelve. His demeanor was neither confident nor abject, but carefully neutral. Only his eyes reflected the hyper alertness of someone aware of mortal danger.

The old man switched from Pashtun to Farsi.

"What is your name?"

"Ziaullah sir."

"I am Mullah Abdullah Khalid, the elder of this village."

The boy put his hands together and bowed.

The old man went on:

"The men who were murdered in the mountain camp were my sons. Under pain of death you will tell me what you know about this - do you understand?"

"Yes sir."

"Why were you with them?"

"I met your sons near the village of Torkham where they had come to attend the wedding of their friend. They allowed me to travel with them as they returned to you here."

"Who killed them?"

"We had stopped for the night and made camp in a mountain pass. They sent me to find fodder for the horses as they were preparing a meal. The attack came from the sky, one of the machines that circle and watch. It fired a rocket into the midst of them."

"Did you see it?"

"I saw it as I was gathering some grass. It was sunset and its shadow passed over the rocks near me. I looked up and saw it hovering high above. I didn't realize what it was until it fired the rocket. It came down low over the camp after that, then it went away".

"What did you do then?"

"I went back to the camp, but a man was there. I had never seen him before. He vanished a moment later."

"He vanished?"

"He was there, and then he was not. I didn't even blink and he was gone!"

"Did you speak to him?"

"Yes, he startled me. Everything in the camp was destroyed, everyone was dead, but this man was there, and not even one hair of his head had been harmed. He was talking but there was nobody there to hear him. I thought he was talking to me – so I asked him who he was."

“Did he answer you?”

“He just stared at me for a moment, then said ‘I am Praggles.’”

“What does that mean?”

“I do not know - he said it, then he disappeared. He did not run away, or hide himself. One instant he was before me and the next instant he was not.”

The Walk-in

AS ABDUR SPOKE, ARGO REMEMBERED his excitement when Abigail Schwartz, a hospital administrator acquaintance who managed a residency program, had asked him to treat the young doctor. As a member of the Pakistani community and a Muslim, Abdur was a very unlikely client. For people of his background seeing a therapist was an extremely rare occurrence, and a certain source of additional problems if discovered. Treating Abdur would give Argo a glimpse into a culture that psychotherapists rarely see, but might also entail unexpected consequences.

Abigail had stated that Abdur was experiencing a crisis of some sort that was affecting his clinical work so badly that he had been ordered to seek counseling as a condition of remaining in the residency program. Argo wondered if he was there only because of the gun being held to his head. This was their first session.

The beginning of the session had been polite and formal. Abdur's comportment and demeanor conveyed intelligence, poise, and maturity - only the perspiration on his forehead indicated discomfort. He spoke easily as Argo queried him for the background information that would become the basis for their work together. Abdur had immigrated to New York with his parents and siblings when he was four years old. His father was a physician, and expected his son to follow in his footsteps. Abdur had been an excellent student, and had gone on to medical school after college as his father wished. He had completed med school the year before, and secured a residency at the hospital where Abigail worked. Abdur had lived with his parents until a month ago, when he'd taken an apartment near the hospital. He stated that he came to Argo at the recommendation of the administrator of the residency program, but failed to mention that he had been compelled to seek treatment.

Abdur's background seemed typical for a young man from that part of the world; he had been raised in a strongly patriarchal family where respect and obedience for parents and grandparents was mandated, and where Muslim religious faith and practice were strongly interwoven into the fabric of the both the family and community. Issues were settled within the family, and failing that, by consulting with the Imam. Argo was satisfied with the baseline information, and re-directed the focus of the session.

"Abdur, I'd like you to tell me now what has brought you here. Take your time, and tell me everything that is of concern."

Abdur squirmed uncomfortably in his seat, and cleared his throat several times before speaking.

"Dr. Masters, I am not sure how to begin, but to say that my life seems to have been turned upside down. If I tell you that everyone I have ever relied upon has turned against me - I would not be exaggerating."

Argo nodded in the affirmative.

"That sounds very upsetting. Can you tell me more about it?"

Abdur responded without hesitation.

"Three years ago I asked my parents for permission to marry a woman I had been seeing since beginning med school. We had fallen in love, and longed to be married and start a family. My father refused to give his blessing, and demanded that I break off the relationship. I pleaded with him to just meet her, but he would not give an inch! I appealed to my mother to intercede, but she would not and urged me to do as my father wished. It was very difficult, but I ended the relationship."

Argo found himself struggling to suppress any telltale signs of how much what Abdur related affected his own emotions. He had been full of rebellion and defiance from adolescence well into his adult life, and even now, stories like this triggered surges of anger within him.

"Did your parents explain why they would not give you their blessing?"

Abdur simply shook his head.

"That must have been a very rough time for you. Did you consider marrying without their permission?"

Abdur became quiet for a moment, then responded:

“Not at that time. It might be difficult for you to understand, but in my culture and religion one does not disobey the wishes of their father or grandfather. At that time, acting against my parent’s wishes was inconceivable.”

Argo reflected back to Abdur:

“Tell me if I’ve got this right. You have pursued a career in medicine in accordance with your parent’s wishes. During medical school you met and fell in love with a woman. The relationship blossomed to the point where the two of you agreed that marriage was the next step. When you requested permission to wed from your parents, they directed you to break off the relationship. That was very difficult for you, but you complied. Is that accurate?”

Abdur nodded.

“Yes, but that is only the beginning. I went on with my studies and graduated from medical school. Last year I began a residency at the general hospital here and met a very distinguished young woman resident who had joined the program the year before me. She is also from Pakistan. She is from a good family, and is a brilliant doctor. We are in love. Two months ago I asked my parents for permission to marry, and once again they have refused. I have taken the step of speaking with the Imam at our mosque, but he counsels me to be patient and to not go against my parents.”

As Abdur described the conflict, Argo could feel his jaw muscles tightening. Given his own rebelliousness as an adolescent, he had been amazed by the diligent acceptance of parental direction in orthodox communities in general.

He had no doubt how he would have behaved in similar circumstances. It had given him an even deeper appreciation of the depth of his own defiant nature. Argo watched as more beads of sweat formed on Abdur's forehead, and heard a quickening in his breathing. He decided to press directly on the sore spot:

"Will you end this relationship?"

Abdur shook his head slowly.

"No, I will not...yet it may be out of my hands. I have moved out of my parent's home and taken an apartment. I have ceased to worship at the Mosque, and am trying to determine how to continue in my faith."

Argo queried: "How is your fiancé handling this crisis?"

The look of misery on Abdur's face previewed his words.

"My actions have created a scandal in our community, and soiled the good name of my fiancé's family and mine as well. They are very upset and have demanded that she break off her relationship with me, leave the residency program and return to Pakistan. She is caught in the middle. One day she was a promising resident in a top program, in love and planning to marry a fellow doctor. Next she is being ostracized in her family and community and being told to give up everything she has worked her whole life to accomplish. The level of stress is unbearable!"

"Are you concerned that she may harm herself?"

Abdur's response was without reservation: "No. It is not how she handles problems."

Argo wondered if Abigail had sent Abdur to him because of their conversations about spiritual matters. They had met and become friends at an inter-faith discussion group. She knew of his fascination with theology and spiritual matters. Argo sat very quietly, allowing voltage to build up in his client's listening.

"Abdur, it is time for you to step back from this situation and get some perspective. Both you and your fiancé have been superb performers in very structured family, cultural, educational and work settings. You have navigated skillfully and diligently to live within the constraints placed upon you, and have achieved a level of academic and career success that is extraordinary by any standards. Neither of you are children any longer, and it is natural that you wish to assume control of your adult lives. Your parents are not in agreement with the choices you have made, and have demanded obedience to their wishes instead. I can understand that you may feel like you are now between a rock and a hard place. Because I respect your ability as a problem solver and an adult, I will not offer you a prescriptive solution, but have a recommendation. May I suggest a course of action to you?"

Abdur hesitated, as if fearful of what Argo would say.

"How can I not listen? This is what I came for."

Argo spoke: "I would like you and your fiancé to spend a week away from the hospital and New York City; some place where you can get some peace and quiet, without being disturbed by anyone. I will speak with Abigail

Schwartz about arranging a short sabbatical for you both. During that week I would like you to meditate on a commandment shared by the Jewish, Christian, and Muslim faiths: 'Honor your mother and your father.' Are you willing to do that?"

Anger spread across Abdur's features: "So you are saying that I should follow my parent's wishes?"

Argo leaned forward and stared directly into Abdur's eyes: "What I would like you to notice is that the commandment does not say 'obey', it says 'honor'. Do you understand the difference?"

Abdur responded. "Honor implies obedience."

Argo proceeded: "Let me flesh it out a bit. If my father directs me to do that which ultimately will be harmful, do I honor him by obeying? If I disobey my father with the intention of creating an outcome that will produce much good, even for him, do I dishonor him? Inquiring in this manner leaves open the possibility of honoring your parents, but allows you to slip out of the straight-jacket of blind obedience."

Abdur's demeanor had softened as Argo spoke, as if a little crack of light had invaded a dark space.

"Do you really think you could arrange a sabbatical from the program for us?"

From Argo's perspective Abigail had very little choice, she was going to lose these two if she didn't.

"I believe so. Do you have a place you can go where nobody will bother you?"

Abdur nodded: "Yes, as a matter of fact we do!"

Argo wrapped up the session.

"I will ask Abigail to contact you with the explicit permission tomorrow. I think it would be best for us to meet again when you return."

Argo stood up to signal that the session was complete. Abdur rose from his seat, and Argo walked him to the door.

As he watched Abdur exit to the outside hallway Argo was startled to notice a man sitting in his waiting room. He had not scheduled any other clients. He had not heard anyone enter the waiting room during his session with Abdur, nor had the doorman called to say he was sending anyone up. The unexpected visitor was tall, fiftyish, with a full head of well-groomed black hair and appeared slim and wiry beneath an immaculately tailored black suit. A black overcoat lay on the couch beside him. His gaze was direct, intense and without a hint of discomfort. He rose from his seat and extended his hand to Argo.

"Dr. Masters, I'm Don Praggles. We spoke yesterday. I've been looking forward to our meeting."

His handshake was firm, and his hands were unusually cold. Argo remembered their phone call the day before, but was sure they had not scheduled a session. He made a snap decision to see him.

"Come in." Argo replied.

It was Argo who felt uncomfortable, and he began the process of self-examination - monitoring and examining his reactions to Praggles. His emotional response to a client was often a valuable tool in evaluating their issues; like a sixth sense that provided early warnings. He motioned toward the couch.

"Please be seated, and let's talk about what brings you here."

Praggles sat and faced Argo, gazing at him as if listening to some invisible dialog between them.

Argo sensed it would be best to forgo the usual small talk. He met Praggles' gaze, and began by summarizing their phone conversation of the prior day.

"You told me that you wished to discuss some issues that have come up related to your business. I recollect you mentioning a need to gain clarity about some changed circumstances related to your work. Can you flesh that out for me?"

Praggles' eyes seemed to be focused on a spot somewhere directly behind him, yet his response was immediate.

"Yes. I am an artisan and work in a very old and specialized domain. I have been experiencing changes and alterations in my workplace that are disturbing to me, and I need to work through them...as you say." He paused for effect then went on.

"I am very, very good at what I do. I cannot remember a time when I wasn't; yet now others intrude into what I have always considered my domain. I need to understand how to address this."

Although Argo could not detect a change in volume or tone in Praggles' voice, and only a slight narrowing of his eyes, he could feel palpable anger and frustration behind his words. Praggles' ability to project his emotional state was as powerful as any Argo had ever experienced; it was a phenomenon he had encountered only with severely psychotic clients.

Argo reflected back: "You have devoted yourself to your craft over a lifetime, it is special work for which you are unusually well suited, and which you have executed with great skill. A competitor or competitors have emerged recently, and, as a result, you perceive shifts and alterations in the landscape of your profession. These changes are upsetting and you wish to get some traction in dealing with them. Is that accurate?"

Argo watched Praggles with a therapist's eye; clients often said more with body language than words. He continued to feel an intense emotional projection.

Praggles was completely motionless, but his eyes focused on Argo in a strangely enervating way.

"These people could put me out of business..." then almost in a whisper: "the consequences could be unimaginable."

Argo replied: "It is clear that this weighs heavily on you. Your choice to seek assistance in dealing with it is a wise one. May I ask what led you to me?"

Praggles tilted his head slightly to one side; his face wore an expression that indicated his new client was observing him closely.

"Of course you would want to know that. You cannot yet fully appreciate what I am going to say, but let me assure you that my search for the right person with whom to discuss these matters has been exhaustive. Of all the possible candidates, you are the best fit."

He stopped speaking and nodded his head as if affirming his own statement.

Argo was having difficulty imagining what Praggles meant, but knew it would be instructive to know more about this:

"Can you be more specific in terms of the criteria you used in making your selection?"

"There is no single quality that I require, but a particular combination. You possess an extraordinary ability to suspend judgment, and enter the experience of your clients. You have an appreciation for spiritual matters and issues both theologically and at an intuitive level, and you possess an intense curiosity to learn and understand human behavior. You have keen moral instincts. These are rounded out by several other qualities; a sense of the gap between what you know and what there is to know; and a willingness to do anything to fill it. You are willing to take great risks in your explorations, and finally – you do not have strong ambitions in the areas of wealth and fame."

Argo was stunned by Praggles' statement. It had been delivered with the clarity of a confident expert, yet there was no way that he could know these things. He sensed that a bland therapeutic response would be grossly inauthentic.

"Exhaustive was a very accurate adjective for your search; a psychic could not have provided a better description. At some point you will have fill me in on how you acquired this information."

In order to keep the focus of the session on Praggles, he decided to postpone exploring how his new client had arrived at his assessment.

"This is our first session, and we will need to begin the process by taking your personal history; that will allow me to get to know you and better understand the goals you seek to achieve in treatment. Some of the information may seem mundane, but please bear with me. It is an important part of the process."

Praggles looked as if he were formulating something to say – for the first time Argo detected hesitation.

"Dr. Masters... it is this history taking that will be the most challenging part of our work together. It will be very hard at first for you to relate to what I will tell you, but you will overcome that. I have never disclosed anything about myself to anyone, ever. I have never seen that as necessary, but understand that for our work this must now occur."

Praggles' discomfort about disclosure brought back a memory of a psychoanalytic lecture Argo had attended where the lecturer, an analyst with fifty years of experience, was asked if there were any clients he would turn away. The old analyst had straight away replied:

"I don't take mafia and I don't take lawyers."

Was Praggles someone he would choose not to treat or did he want to discuss issues which Argo would be ethically required to report?

"My concern is not that I cannot relate to you, but I want you to understand the confidentiality issues here. Whatever we discuss will remain between us with one exception. I have an obligation, as a licensed therapist, to report any credible, expressed intention by a client to harm another or himself. Do you understand that?"

Praggles sat completely still, yet Argo could feel him struggling.

"That will not be a problem. It is my personal history and identity that will present you with the biggest challenges. But I am certain you will overcome them. The problem is twofold; the content of my history is most unusual, but there is more. It has been a very, very long time since I have attempted to express myself honestly or authentically, and request your forbearance as I do so."

Every nerve ending in Argo's body sensed danger, but he proceeded. He needed to understand what Praggles had just said.

"I appreciate your confidence in me, but would like to clarify what you have said about never expressing yourself honestly and authentically."

Praggles chose his words carefully:

"My relationships with people have been of two types, business and ah...administrative. My business communications subordinate everything to the goals of the business. The administrative part, being the boss, is similar; it's all about the business. I have never sought an authentic dialog with any human being."

Argo was getting an almost psychedelic, other worldly vibe from what Praggles had said, and wondered at the emphasis he had placed on 'human being'. He formulated his next reflection to open that up.

"Your life and every relationship you have had up until now has been strictly about business. You have reached an impasse in conducting your business and have chosen to seek assistance in formulating a new approach. Collaborating with another is new territory for you, and you see that it will require communicating in a manner wholly unfamiliar to you. You are struggling with this. I would like you to help me understand how this came to be so. Every human being has parents, and it is there that you must have had intimate, interpersonal communications. Can you describe a typical communication you had with your mother or father?"

Praggles stared at Argo like a diver about to leave the high board for the first time. Even though he never seemed to move, Argo could feel a rush of energy coming from him. He leaned forward and widened his eyes allowing Argo to gaze into a strange, bottomless chaos.

"The point is, Dr. Masters, I am not human – I am a spiritual being. I am referred to in the various scriptures as 'Satan'."

Argo listened to Praggles with his ears, eyes and psychic senses. Although he felt completely overwhelmed, he maintained his therapist like composure. In treating psychotic clients, one does not challenge their delusions head-on at first. He now understood his own emotional turmoil; Praggles, like many severely psychotic patients, had the ability to project his emotional state onto those around him. The turmoil that now filled him originated with Praggles. Argo knew he was not the right therapist for this client, and must now figure out how to steer him to someone who could really help him.

"Don, that makes sense to me now. When you spoke of never communicating intimately with a human being, without the spiritual context I was left wondering about such things as parents, siblings, aunts, uncles, etc. What puzzles me at this point is how to proceed. My training is in dealing with human issues. What similarities are there between human and spiritual beings? What differences should I be aware of?"

Praggles demeanor was cold and businesslike:

"I will answer your question Dr. Masters even knowing that you believe me to be psychotic and delusional. Once you understand I am whom I say, you will appreciate how hard I am working to communicate with you. The answer to your question requires knowledge of being and spirituality that you already possess. It is one of the reasons I chose you. Are you ready to hear my answer?"

Argo had not expected Praggles' response, and knew he would have to listen very carefully for clues to the architecture of what confronted him. He nodded.

"Spiritual beings come from the Creator. They are not corporeal, although some may assume that state temporarily."

He briefly paused and motioned to himself, then continued.

"They do not have what you refer to as a childhood; they are created fully capable to perform their function. Newly created spiritual beings possess the quality you call innocence, which diminishes with the passing of time. Spiritual beings are created with a purpose, and never...ah...or almost never, give any thought to deviating from that purpose. There are many types of spiritual beings, and hierarchies exist both within and between the types. Is there anything I've said so far that does not agree with the understanding you possess?"

Argo had been so completely absorbed in Praggles' exposition that he was startled by the question, and decided to push back a little. Argo wanted to press Praggles to a point where he would begin to reveal the psychotic underpinnings of his delusions.

"It does agree and it raises one question for me. May I ask you something?"

Praggles nodded.

"Spiritual beings are created with a purpose and do not deviate from it, or rarely deviate from it. Satan is reputed to have deviated – to have rebelled against his creator. Does this have any bearing on your decision to seek counseling?"

Argo felt as if he had stepped on a live wire, whatever was going on with his client was affecting him at a physical level. Praggles' gaze seemed to be turned inward and he did not respond for almost a minute, when he did his voice was measured but not calm.

"The only deviation is my presence here. What has been perceived as my rebellion is ahhh...not accurate. I have always done exactly what I was created to do - until now."

Argo knew he had hit a nerve; everything in Praggle's demeanor reflected an inner conflict. He searched for the intervention that would prompt his client to reveal more, but his mind felt numb. Argo was suddenly aware of being very cold, and incredibly weary.

Praggles stood, and walked to a spot directly in front of him.

"My presence is draining for you, and you have become exhausted. I am going to leave you now, and will return at the same time next week. During this week, I will help you accept what is before you. When you accept me, our work will begin."

Praggles removed an envelope from his vest pocket and placed it on Argo's desk.

"Read this after I leave."

Praggles went to the door, and turned to Argo.

"Until next week, Dr. Masters."

Argo did not hear the outer door to the waiting room close, and went out to see if Praggles was lingering there. He wasn't. He returned to his office and opened the envelope. There was a single sheet of white paper containing a clear handwritten script that read:

Dr. Masters,

The physical and mental suffering you experience as a result of being in my presence will pass within several hours, and have no lasting effect. This note is to aid in your transition from disbelief. When I return next week we will complete the process, and can then begin the work we must do. When I revealed myself as we conversed, you had no choice but to search for a psychoanalytic, delusional cubbyhole in which to place me. Your reaction today was anticipated. You will move past this obstacle. Only then will you be able to assist in the work at hand.

What follows are three items: an answer to a theological question that has long puzzled you, then a brief summary of an event which is not known by anyone but you, and finally a prophesy concerning a client of yours. It is said that everyone has a price, and in my work that has been proven to be an immutable fact. You have a thirst for spiritual knowledge Dr. Masters, and my payment to you will be in that currency. Item one below is the first installment.

The Tower of Babel. The most prevalent belief concerning this scripture is that it was the act of a jealous God to prevent mankind from usurping his power. You have never been comfortable with that interpretation. You intuitively reject the idea that the creator would impede men from communicating for the betterment of humanity. The common interpretation of the scripture is completely incorrect. Reinterpret it from this certain knowledge: If mankind were granted unbridled, universal communication, they would destroy themselves.

When you were 22 years old, driving on a rainy night, a disembodied voice commanded you to take actions that surely saved your life. It prevented you from being in a fatal automobile crash. You never mentioned this experience to anyone.

Although you experience strong sexual countertransference with one of your clients; you are quite certain you would never cross the line and use your relationship as a therapist for seduction. Think again doctor.

Till our next meeting.

Argo slumped face down on his desk.

He did not remember losing consciousness, but his watch read 12:45am. He had been out cold for several hours. Argo wasn't sure he'd ever felt this badly - even in his heavy drinking days. The oppressive physical misery accompanied by a torturous, hopeless depression seemed to stretch unendingly from the past to now, and then on into a future of unrelieved bleakness. He kicked himself up from his desk, exited his office, went through the small waiting room, down the hall to the elevator and pressed the down button. He knew better than to let this mental state paralyze him; he needed to keep moving.
First he would speak to the doorman about not letting people up to the floor unannounced, and then decide what to do about his new client. The elevator door opened and Argo hurried through the lobby to the doorman's station. Phil stood behind the desk and peered inquiringly at him.

"Phil, I had a client come up to the office unannounced at about 10PM. Did he sign in?"

Phil replied: "The young fella who went up about 9PM is the last person I sent up to you Dr. Masters."

Argo was frustrated: "No Phil, after him there was a tall, slender man with very sharp facial features – about my age. Do you know who I'm talking about?"

Phil seemed upset that Argo didn't get what he was saying: "No Dr. Masters, like I said, the young guy was the last person I sent up."

Argo replied: "Let me see the sign in log, maybe he said he was seeing someone else."

Phil was emphatic: "Dr. Masters, he was the last person who came through this lobby; it's been a very quiet night here. If there is someone up there who shouldn't be there, maybe we should call the police and have them search the place."

Argo decided to let it go: "This puzzles me Phil, but it is possible he was one of the people who live on the upper floors. He didn't seem menacing or dangerous in any way. I'm sure I'll get to the bottom of it. Sorry to trouble you – I'm going up to turn the lights out, and then I'm calling it a night."

He returned to his office and started a new file for Praggles. He thought a moment, and then printed 'Dark Red' where the client's name usually went. He had an intuition that treating Praggles would be a dark redemption of some sort. He made some case notes, placed them in the file, then went home and slept.

Argo

VERY FEW PEOPLE KNEW HOW HE HAD come to be called Argo. Those who thought about it at all presumed it was derived from the Argonauts of the Greek mythological stories of Jason and the Golden Fleece. In fact it began as a nickname among his friends because of his angry, rebelliousness as a teenager. There was a knock, knock joke at the time that went:

> Knock, knock.
> Who's there?
> Argo.
> Argo who?
> Argo f_ _ _ yourself.

With time he had lost the angry edge, but the name had stuck. Argo was a man who took little at face value – a seeker and questioner. He listened to people but was always sure to note if their feet took them to the same places their mouths did. Being a therapist was his second career; he had transitioned to it as a result of personal transformational experiences that inspired him to spend the balance of his life assisting others in finding their paths.

Argo practiced psychotherapy in New York City from an office in a high-rise on the Western edge of Hell's

Kitchen. It had sweeping views looking up the Hudson River and Northern Manhattan. The office was decorated simply, the waiting room was softly lit, with two couches facing each other, a coffee table in the middle with magazines, and a copy of Van Gogh's Starry Night on the wall. The inner office was similarly decorated, except for a big window. Argo loved the view; he secretly held the belief that people thought bigger if they could see farther.

He possessed a warm and empathetic nature, as well as a demeanor that was outwardly calm, even when he wasn't. His patients tended to adore him and were uniformly convinced he possessed extraordinary wisdom and insight. Few suspected these gifts had been acquired the hard way; digging out from under the consequences of hard early, and not so early, life choices and circumstances. His ability to empathize was often enhanced by the first hand understanding of someone who had been there too.

He had been a sensitive, whimsical, headstrong child with a tendency toward rebellion that became more pronounced as he approached adolescence. His mother and father were both strong personalities; smart, willful and incompatible. As their household swelled with children, unforeseen financial reversals and health issues cracked open the fault lines in their relationship. Argo's once secure and orderly family gradually morphed into something that seemed chaotic and unrecognizable to him. At the age of thirteen, in a cloud of youthful resentment, he had declared his parents unfit to raise him. He couldn't leave; so he simply never listened to them again. They reached out to him, but he would not budge.

Many teenage children become disenchanted with their parents. It is likely that in time Argo would have resolved his issues with them, but fate had other plans. His father died suddenly when he was eighteen, and his mother passed away a year later. For two people he had professed to despise, they left an enormous, empty hole in his life. It wasn't till they were gone; that he realized how much he loved them. The tears he shed for them were the last that would fall from his eyes for a very long time.

He watched helplessly as his family disintegrated. His two younger sisters were sent away to boarding school by Aunts and Uncles who had no idea what else to do with them. He and his two younger brothers had to fend for themselves, and went in separate directions. His youngest brother Bill moved in with a friend's family and worked in their store after school and on weekends. His brother Franklin was seventeen, and was given permission to enlist. He joined the Marines. Argo found a job as a laborer in an iron foundry. Each of them had been scarred by the tragedy that had overtaken their family and would carry its darkness forward. Bad news never surprised Argo; he was certain that he and every member of his family were cursed.

Argo's view of what was possible in life was colored by what he had seen. If asked, he'd probably have spoken stirringly about admiring resourcefulness and self-reliance. In truth he saw these qualities as necessary to his survival, believing himself completely alone. His choice to push away from his parents became a model for all his relationships. He even jettisoned God; discarding his childhood religious training, and adopting a strident atheism. He felt terribly alone, but could not see that he was the source of his own isolation.

He enrolled in a community college and began his studies as an evening student. One night while driving home from classes an incident occurred that Argo could neither explain nor find a context. The school was twenty miles away. It was a cold and rainy night, which seemed to swallow up the illumination of his headlights in its blackness. He was leaving the thruway and entering a one-lane ramp that wound down through a ravine to a local parkway. He was traveling sixty miles per hour, and peering intently at the blackness ahead when a voice startled him.

"Stop the car!" it said.

He knew he was alone, but spun around to check the back seat, then tested the knob on the radio to see if it was somehow 'on' – it wasn't. He had not slowed down, and the voice commanded him again.

"Stop the car NOW!"

The authority in the voice was so compelling that Argo braked and brought the car to a halt in the middle of the ramp. The outlines of an enormous boulder blocking the road appeared before him. He had no explanation for the voice, but knew that his life would have ended without its intervention. He never related the incident to anyone because there was no explanation that made any sense to him.

On the surface Argo's life seemed to progress. The job at the foundry became a desk job. A year later he was selected to participate in a company-training program in technology and became a computer programmer. He met a young woman who was an office temp at his firm, and they dated. She was puzzled by the barriers to intimacy Argo put up, but was sure she would eventually overcome them. They married several years later, and during the next five years they had three children, two girls and a boy. His children were the only people on earth he could express his love to freely. He loved them so much it brought tears to his eyes. He was determined to be a good father.

Argo completed a bachelor's degree, and changed jobs, securing a position working in technology for an investment bank in New York. After a few more years he started his own consulting business. He specialized in applications for the investment-banking sector. The work amused him; it was like a huge Monopoly Game controlling and tracking the movements of hundreds of billions of dollars. Argo had a keen mind and an ability to grasp the most complex system architectures, and was easily able to provide a good living for his family by marketing this knowledge.

Just as it is impossible to build a sturdy home on a poor foundation, no matter how far a person comes in life, they have to deal with their ghosts. Argo accumulated more and more trappings of a successful adult life, but the solitary emptiness inside him grew. A lifetime of unresolved feelings and conflicts lurked just beneath the surface. He utilized alcohol to manage them, but every year it took a little more. By age 35 his drinking had become the central feature of his life. It happened so gradually that he had been able to ignore its effects. His family had learned not to disturb him in the evenings, and up until the end he was able to function at work. The breaking point came when his oldest daughter had a crisis and came to him for help one evening after he had returned from the office. She was 14 and was starting at a new school. She felt unwelcome and terribly isolated there. As she tried to tell Argo about her feelings, panic overtook him. He drank himself into a blackout. How could he deal with her feelings when he was unable to handle his own? When he awoke the next day, and realized what had happened, he knew he had hit bottom. His children were truly the only connection he had, and failing them was not an option. He skipped lunch that day to attend his first AA meeting. It was the beginning of his recovery from alcoholism and from the thinking that had helped him become one.

Early in his recovery, he realized it wasn't just about his not drinking. He had believed that alcohol was what had made life bearable, blotting out the emptiness and sorrow. He knew now that the desolation was inside of him, not part of the external world, and that he would need every molecule of his brain functioning if he wished to escape it. The AA meetings were definitely helping him connect with his feelings and lose his sense of isolation, but he hungered for more. A vision was slowly forming within him of a life he could mold into something extraordinary. He wanted to accelerate the process in any way he could. There is an old saying 'When the student is ready, the teacher will appear.' Argo couldn't have been more ready.

He began working with a therapist named George who was also an alcoholic and had been in recovery for twenty years. There was something wonderful about George, he radiated happiness and laughter no matter what life handed him. George and Argo spent the first three session getting acquainted and reviewing the events of his life. At the end of the third session he told Argo that their next meeting would be two hours long, and he should come prepared to work. When Argo asked him what that meant, George just smiled and told Argo not to be concerned about understanding the therapeutic techniques - just surrender to them.

"Trust me."

The next session was not what Argo had expected, in fact it seemed downright weird; he kept waiting for something dramatic to happen, but it never did. George began the session by lowering the lights, and instructing Argo to sit comfortably in his chair with his hands turned palms up in his lap, and his eyes closed. He guided Argo through some relaxation meditations for a few moments. He then told Argo that he was going to help him build a special room; in this room Argo could summon anyone with whom he wished to speak. For the balance of the two hours, he directed Argo to wield an imaginary hammer and nails to construct the details of the 'room'. He walked him through connecting the studs and beams, and laying the flooring. George guided Argo through the process of paneling the walls, and building a sacred doorway. This doorway would be the place where those with whom Argo desired to speak would appear. The detail with which George insisted Argo build the room seemed ridiculous, but he did as he was told. After two hours, George announced that their time was up and the session was over. Argo was very confused.

One week later, Argo showed up for his appointment with George, and again the lights were turned down. George instructed Argo as he had the week before: sit comfortably, hands in his lap, palms up, and eyes closed. When Argo had done that, George again guided him through a relaxing meditation for a few moments. He then instructed Argo to go into the special room he had built the week before, and to sit quietly before the sacred door. Once again he told Argo that when he opened the door, the person or people he needed to speak with would be there. Argo had no idea who he wanted to talk to, but thought to himself: "I've gone this far, I might was well continue."

George instructed Argo to open the door. Argo imagined himself reaching over, placing his hand on the knob he had installed just the week before, turning it and pulling the door open.

Before him, sitting side by side, with a vividness bolder than in life, were his mother and father. They gazed at him lovingly, silently. A sob rose out of Argo. It seemed to start in his toes and passed wrenchingly upward through his entire body. Many others followed it. Tears flowed from his eyes so rapidly that they ran down his face and soaked his collar. He could not control the wracking sobs; he held himself and rocked back and forth and cried and cried. He saw and felt in an instant the power of the love he had always had for them. It was stronger than anything he remembered having felt before. It had been concealed intact within him for every minute of his life since he buried it and them so many years ago. When he was finally able to talk, he told George who he was speaking to. George nodded, and asked:

"Do you have anything you would like to say to them?"

Argo looked at his parents and uttered:

"I am so sorry, I am so, so sorry, please forgive me for being so awful to you. I always loved you, I just couldn't show it."

Their faces shown with a soft radiance. The serenity and love in their eyes needed no words – it was the nourishment his soul had craved. Gradually the image of Argo's parents faded away. He opened his eyes. George got him a glass of water, and tissues to sop up the tears still on his face and neck. He was weak, joyous, and mystified, all at the same time. Argo told George he was completely stunned at the depth of love and feeling for his mother and father that had poured forth from him. He had been completely unaware of its presence.

George gazed at Argo for a moment, then quietly continued.

"It was clear you had buried the memory and love of your parents, and that doing so had cost your emotional soul. How could you ever express love toward yourself or anyone else after denying the relationships that were the source of your life? Argo, you have some work to do my friend. Do you think your parents are the only ones you've buried?"

Argo worked with George for several years. The catharsis and healing he experienced opened up both his heart and his mind, and he was filled with an unquenchable enthusiasm for life and a hunger for knowledge. His atheism had given way to an intuitive belief in a higher power, mostly as a result of attending AA meetings. Again and again he saw miraculous recoveries – people snatched from the gates of oblivion by a grace he could only identify as divine. His atheism had been like his relationship with his parents - he had buried God like he had buried them. One Easter Sunday his wife insisted that he accompany her and the children to church. He did and was profoundly moved by the pastor's sermon. Serendipitously he was invited to attend a weekly men's bible study. He found reading the scriptures and seeking to understand their meaning completely engrossing. Argo attended the men's bible study for several years, but gradually came to feel that a deeper understanding was possible. The studies he attended seemed to reduce a magnificent and unknowable God into bite sized chunks more suitable for children's intellects. He wanted more, and sought out scholarly studies that combined theological inquiry with a historical and critical analysis. He became quite conversant in theological issues. The study of spiritual matters is rarely conclusive, but Argo never tired of examining and contemplating them.

Argo came to realize that his interests did not lie in the area of investment banking or computer systems. He was fascinated with the idea of helping people find a way to live satisfying and fulfilling lives. His transformation from a bitter, nihilistic alcoholic had shown him what was possible. Argo's everyday experience with people in business, at AA meetings, socially and at the church convinced him that many people were capable of such a transformation. He began to explore ways in which he could facilitate others in making the transition. Argo lacked the education to go into the helping professions, but knew that is where he belonged. He spoke with his wife, and asked how she felt about him attending evening and weekend classes to obtain the education he would need to transition to a new way of making a living. She had no objection as long as he continued to support the family. Argo began immediately. Twelve years later, he hung out his shingle as a licensed psychotherapist.

All the studying, classes, internships and other work that Argo did to prepare himself for his new career was done while working full time to support his family. He and his wife slowly developed separate lives. While they seemed quite cordial, increasingly their lives and interests diverged. Argo and his wife divorced the same year he established his practice, the millennium. She had married a very different man than Argo had become. He cared deeply for his wife, but knew their paths had parted to a degree they could never be joined again. Argo sensed it would be better to ride out this period, than return to a marriage that would never satisfy either of them. He often felt like a fraud - facilitating life transformations for his clients, while his own family suffered through the chaos of a divorce. He and his now ex-wife tried to work together out of the bond of love they shared for the children. Argo came to admire her resilience and the way she created a new life for herself. He developed a loving relationship with a woman who helped him through this period. She was divorced too, and although the love they shared was vibrant and sustaining, neither could convince the other that marriage was a good idea. At various times one would propose it, but always the other was wary - three months later they would have the same discussion, but the roles would be reversed. The lack of a marriage certificate didn't lessen their passion for each other.

Argo's first office space was on the ninth floor of building 5 of the World Trade Center Complex. On the morning of September 11, 2001, he had gone in early to handle some insurance claim paperwork, and was at his desk when the first plane struck the North Tower. After hearing what sounded like an enormous explosion, he went to the window of his office, which looked out on the courtyard in the complex's center. He jumped back when something the size of a small car smashed into the courtyard from above, and exploded into fragments that flew outward from the impact. What followed was so much falling debris that Argo could not even see the South Tower across the courtyard. In the hallway outside his office nobody had any idea what was happening, but it was clear they needed to evacuate. Argo ran to an emergency stairwell and clambered down to the second floor lobby that had exits to both the central courtyard and Church St. He stopped there to take one last look at the debris filled courtyard. It was a decision he would forever regret. Unbeknownst to Argo, over thirteen hundred people had been in the North Tower at and above the ninety third floor where the plane had struck. Everyone between the ninety third and ninety eighth floors was killed instantly. Those in the floors above were trapped - the plane had destroyed the emergency evacuation stairwells. They faced a ghastly choice as the floors they occupied filled with flames and smoke – jump or burn. At first Argo did not understand what he was witnessing, but as the horror of it tried to sink into his consciousness, his senses shut down to protect him from the nightmare. He was guided out the Church Street exit by police managing the evacuation, and joined the throngs marching away from the Trade Center. He was several blocks away from the site when the second plane struck the South Tower. Up until that instant, nobody had been sure what was happening, but a sudden and simultaneous realization that they were under attack swept through everyone present - as it did with those watching around the world.

It would take many months for Argo to reconstruct the events of that morning. The images of the doomed victims falling never came back; he was grateful for that. The September 11th attacks awakened an awareness of evil. He had been preoccupied with his own struggles against darkness, now a latent fascination with the nature and causes of evil emerged. It started him on a path of inquiry that quickly brought him to the borders of a dreadfully stark world. The paths leading to hatred and slaughter seemed to be multiplying yet remained beyond his understanding. He read the works of some of the most prolific architects of suffering; Lenin's manifestos. Hitler's Mein Kampf and translations of Pol Pot's cold calculus provided an understanding of the heartless logic that drove it. They unabashedly articulated mass murder as a viable method of achieving political goals. During a trip to Prague, he detoured to Poland to visit the remains of the Berkenau and Auschwitz extermination camps. The earth near the crematoriums was still peppered with the bone fragments of victims. He wondered what line a person must cross that makes murder acceptable. Argo had an intuition that his destiny was to be engulfed and do battle in the dark wastelands of horror he now sought to confront.

The Decision

ARGO HAD DECIDED TO TREAT PRAGGLES even before going downstairs to speak with the doorman. He always referred psychotics to practitioners who specialized in their treatment; it was not an area of either competence or interest for him. When he examined the details of Praggles' session, he could find scant evidence of psychosis. Psychotics often have trouble locating themselves in time and space, but Praggles had shown up exactly at the end of his last client's session. Praggles had ended their session by saying he did not require that Argo accept his claimed identity as a hard fact, just that he be open to the possibility. Psychotics, as a rule, see themselves surrounded by people who don't understand them. Praggles had shown an appreciation of how difficult it would be for Argo to accept his statements about himself, and had worked cleverly to dispel his doubts. His attentiveness to Argo's verbal communication and body language had been flawless, and his intuitive understanding of his thought processes had bordered on the clairvoyant.

Praggles' claim of being Satan was outside the realm of anything Argo would have taken seriously, yet there were a number of similarly unexplainable phenomenon Praggles had introduced that tended to support that claim. There was his possession of knowledge for which there was no explanation. He had delivered a description of Argo's psychic makeup of such accuracy that Argo's most intimate acquaintance could not have duplicated it. The first two items in his note to Argo had been spot on. How could Praggles possibly have known of his thoughts about the Tower of Babel scriptures? His reference to the near fatal incident in the car was even more inexplicable. He puzzled about the third item, the prophecy, but sensed he would soon find out.

Perhaps most impressive and disturbing was Praggles' knowledge that Argo would be powerfully motivated by his offer of spiritual knowledge. Argo's thirst for spiritual truth had grown steadily since the beginning of his recovery from alcoholism. He had learned that there were few, if any, hard answers in spiritual inquiries. To study such matters was to rely on analyzing ancient texts, intuition, faith, the experience of other inquirers, guesswork and for the lucky few – revelation. The idea that working with Praggles could provide sought after answers was reason enough to proceed. He sensed something else drawing him in, but was not yet able to articulate it.

He had a few dilemmas to work out. If Praggles turned out to be psychotic, he would have to discover it quickly and refer him elsewhere. He needed to find a way to rule it out. If Praggles was indeed Satan or some other onerous spiritual being, Argo would need to understand two things as quickly as possible: first, what Praggles wished to accomplish in therapy, and second, would Argo be able to assist him without de facto harm being done to others and himself. Argo knew he would have to be two-headed with regard to his responsibility to this client and to those people who could be affected by alterations in his client's psychic circumstances.

Another problem would be finding someone to supervise him in his treatment of Praggles. Tackling a case this challenging without access to the perspective of another capable analyst would be unthinkable. Argo took professional supervision from a wise old therapist named Abe Mack who headed the Mack Institute for Psychoanalytic Studies. Abe ran a lecture and supervision group that met on Saturday mornings, at which time he worked with Argo and other therapists on issues arising in their various practices. Abe was an avowed atheist, and would likely take Argo's new client's claims as prima facie evidence of psychosis. Further, the group supervision format was definitely out of the question for this case. He could think of no one.

Argo had learned that needed answers and insights didn't always come as a result of logical and methodical searching. He spent time each evening in prayer and meditation; sometimes ten minutes and at other times an hour. Argo used the serenity prayer he had learned in AA when he needed to center himself. It was simple and mantra-like, and allowed him to empty his mind of the noisy chatter that usually cluttered it by days end. He would repeat it again and again; seeking to focus on the meaning of each phrase.

Eventually a profound peacefulness would wash over him. He had found answers to many pressing inquiries in that psychic silence, and so it was today. He remembered a Catholic priest, Fr. John, who was trained as a pastoral counselor. They had both attended the same AA meeting when Argo had done an internship in midtown during the last year of his studies. Fr. John had shared eloquently about his battles with alcohol, and often mentioned the cleverness of Satan in bringing him to the brink of ruin. At first his speaking had seemed naïve to Argo, but the insights and wisdom of his observations soon dispelled that notion. Fr. John had come to the priesthood as Argo had come to his profession – via a life transition. He had been a soldier, and been involved in covert actions in Cambodia and Laos. He returned haunted by what he had seen and done; and addicted to alcohol and heroin. He eventually found recovery in the same church basement AA meetings as Argo. His recovery led him to enter the priesthood of the Roman Catholic Church. He had eventually risen to the rank monsignor in the church, but had been reduced to the status of parish priest after an alcoholic relapse. Argo never knew the exact details of his demotion, but remembered being struck by the humility of the priest's acceptance of it. He remembered that Fr. John had been assigned to a small, struggling church on West 37th Street. An Internet search quickly yielded a listing. When he phoned, a woman's voice with a pronounced Irish accent answered: "St. Joseph's parish house, may I help you?"

Argo and Fr. John had agreed to meet an hour later at a coffee shop near Penn Station. Argo got there first, and took a booth that gave him a view of the door. When Fr. John arrived, he caught his eye and waved him over to the booth. The priest had an unremarkable appearance that belied the breadth of his humanity and life experience. As he sat down, he extended his hand in greeting:

"Argo, I haven't seen you since your internship in the drug and alcohol rehab when you were finishing up your graduate degree. You came to the Midtown Group's lunchtime AA meetings then. I trust you're still making meetings?"

Argo assured Fr. John that he was, although he admitted he was down to one or two meetings a week. Argo inquired after the priest's wellbeing, and Fr. John replied that he was still just a simple parish priest, and a grateful, recovering alcoholic. After the waitress took their order, Fr. John focused the conversation:

"So tell me about this client of yours."

Argo took a deep breath and began.

"I had spoken with him by phone a day before he appeared, but we had not scheduled an appointment. He said his name was "Don Praggles," and he showed up at my office yesterday evening promptly after my last scheduled appointment. When I escorted what I thought was my last client out, he was sitting in the waiting room. He appeared to be about fifty years of age, tall, slender but wiry, very well groomed, black hair, his skin was remarkably white and smooth and he wore an impeccably tailored black business suit. I decided to see him and began an intake interview. Are you with me so far?"

The priest nodded and gestured for Argo to continue.

"Immediately my countertransference to him warned me that something was different. There was an energy emanating from him that was new to me. At first I thought he might be schizophrenic, because the emotional projection was so strong and abrasive. The reasons he gave for seeking therapy were trouble dealing with business related stresses connected with new competitors. When I began gathering personal information the interview became difficult. When I pressed, he stopped me and asked that I listen to him for a moment. For the first time in the session, he exhibited real discomfort - then he told me that he was Satan. At that point I was certain he was psychotic, but he had anticipated my response. We spoke for another half hour. I don't know who he is, but he isn't any flavor of psychotic I've encountered before."

Fr. John regarded Argo with raised eyebrows and said nothing for a moment. When he did speak, it was slowly and thoughtfully.

"Argo, if I hadn't gotten to know you by hearing you speak in meetings a number of times over the years, I'd be out the door by now. He sounds insane, and even a bit theatrical. For instance, the name "Don Praggles;" the "Don" would be used in the regal sense and Praggles is an acronym for the seven deadly sins: Pride, Anger, Greed,

Gluttony, Lust, Envy and Sloth. What you are describing seems an open and shut case of severe mental disturbance. Why don't you tell me why you no longer think so?"

Argo was grateful that the priest had not dismissed him. He knew his listener was well versed in the distinctions of counseling and did not need painstaking explanations. He recounted the session's highlights. Praggles' keen sense of time and place, his appreciation of the difficulty Argo would have with his revelation, the thoroughness and accuracy of his knowledge of Argo's psychic profile. He went on to relate Praggles' conversation about the difference between physical beings and spiritual beings. Fr. John listened quietly. Finally, Argo related the session's end, when Praggles had warned him about the drain his presence would have, and the note he handed him as he was leaving. Argo took Praggles' note out of his breast pocket and handed it to the priest.

Fr. John looked at the sheet of paper, examining both sides before handing it back to Argo. There was a troubled look on his face as he spoke:

"You have just handed me a blank sheet of paper. What am I supposed to deduce from that?"

Argo was stunned. He looked at the note; it was as readable now as it had been when Praggles gave it to him. He wondered aloud if Fr. John was beginning to doubt his sanity:

"John, maybe I'm crazy but I am looking at a page crammed with hand written script. You don't see it?"

Fr. John shrugged his shoulders: "I see a blank sheet of paper. Let's do this; read it to me."

Argo complied. As he read the note, Fr. John's demeanor became even more thoughtful. When Argo finished the priest asked him about the second point:

"What is the reference about the near automobile crash? Tell me about it."

Argo related the incident of the disembodied voice that had saved his life by warning him to stop his car on that rainy night many years ago. How he had reluctantly obeyed it, decelerating from sixty miles per hour and rolling to a halt six feet from the huge rock that blocked the road.

Fr. John asked: "Who did you tell about this?"

"I never told anybody, I was afraid they would think I was crazy." Argo replied

Fr. John smiled: "I can see that. Not sure I would have done any differently. What about the last point – the prophecy?"

"I can't imagine what he is referring to," Argo replied.

Fr. John continued: "I don't know what to make of this. You seem to have your feet on the ground, even if what you are relating is very far-fetched. At this point all I can do is offer you my ear as a sounding board. Let's meet again after your client's next visit. Hopefully he's just another psychotic, but on the off chance he isn't, I will share what little information I have about satanic presence. There are a few qualities that seem to be consistent in the experiences related by those who have had contact. The spirit is said to lack the ability to love or even have affection, and despises mankind in its entirety. The sense of being drained could be explained by exposure to that. During exorcisms, the satanic spirit almost always possesses knowledge of the personal lives of those participating in the sacrament. There have also been reports of unexplainable physical manifestations like levitation. Lastly, and this is fairly obvious, Satan is not bound by his word."

The priest stopped speaking for a moment as if weighing his next words.

"Argo, if this turns out to be a satanic contact, it will mean you are in indescribable physical and spiritual danger, even if it does not seem so at the moment. Do you understand that"?

Argo experienced a sudden desire to end the conversation. He had not intended to speak about his motivation.

"John, if he shows up for his next appointment, we can deal with it. I won't be able to see what choices are before me until this proceeds further. For now, let's leave it like that."

As he gathered up his jacket to leave, the priest asked him a question.

"If Praggles does turn out to be who he says, will you continue to treat him?"

The question took Argo by surprise. He knew the priest had sensed something in his demeanor or speaking and was determined to explore it.

"Why do you ask?"

Fr. John cocked his head to one side, and peered at Argo.

"Please listen to me carefully. In the drastically unlikely event that you are being sought out by Satan, you are in more than mortal danger. You are dangling your toes over the proverbial abyss. I sense that you have another agenda, and that is what most concerns me. The only way I can help you is if you are completely open and honest with me. You hope Praggles is Satan. Why?"

He was impressed by the priest's astuteness of observation. He had been awash in ambivalence about his own motives, but tried to explain what he knew so far.

"John, I've spent years pouring over scriptures, studying, listening to lectures on everything from the underpinnings of the trinity to predestination. It fascinates me that he might be able to fill in some of the gaps, but that isn't the thing. All my life I've felt blindsided by dark events. I have been struggling to understand what seem to me to be the colossal forces of evil that surround us. I spent a vacation visiting the death camps in Poland in search of some glimmer of understanding. I've read the historical accounts and the political reasoning behind the slaughter of humanity in Europe in the Second World War, the Soviet Gulags, Cambodia's Killing Fields and the more recent genocides in Europe and Africa. I was in the World Trade Center on September 11th. Without knowing why, I've had a growing premonition that I am somehow meant to confront this or be annihilated by it. Am I deluding myself? Am I just greedy for knowledge that I have no right to? Am I an arrogant fool who doesn't know better than to put himself in the way of a freight train? I can only tell you I'm feeling my way at this point."

There was a long silence before the priest responded.

"I have seen many things in many places that could only have been born of an evil beyond my ability to imagine. You and I are no match for those forces. Frankly, I pray that Praggles is psychotic. You are not Frodo Baggins and this is not some Tolkienesque faceoff with the forces of darkness. There is no possibility that contact with Satan will do anything but provide an opportunity to expand his influence."

Argo heard the priest's words, and waited to be sure he was finished.

"John, I am a man who has made many wrong turns in his early life. As you know, I've moved past that. In doing the work of finding the right path, I've developed a pretty good ability to distinguish my true calling from the noisy cacophony of wishes and desires that often fill my head. I want you to know that I'm drawn to do whatever work there is with regard to Praggles, even knowing it could be exceedingly dangerous – even deadly. It is not my ego, or greed that motivates me. I sense this is what I was born to do; it is my destiny."

The priest said nothing for a moment. From the far-away look in his eyes, it was clear that Argo's statement had affected him.

"I get the sense it is that way for you. I have had a similar feeling, like the other shoe is about to drop and I'll be there when it does. Let me explore this a bit with you. Have you read any of the recent works that have been published about exorcism?"

Argo nodded. "I have and they have been chilling, but we are not dealing with that here. I am not possessed, nor do I have any desires or inclinations that would lead to that outcome. I sense I must participate in an interaction with this being or person; and only then will I discover why."

Fr. John nodded as Argo spoke; he seemed to know that Argo must play this out.

"The Church recognizes that there are instances when contact is necessary. So far this has been limited to the sacrament of exorcism. Satan is much more powerful and clever than any of us, so contact is only initiated after thorough spiritual preparation, and only in the name of Christ. Some very nasty things have occurred to those who have strayed from that protocol. It is not unprecedented for someone outside the priesthood to attempt contact, but it is much more dangerous. What is completely unique about what you have described, it is that contact is being initiated from the other side. If this client of yours is authentic, you will need every molecule of spiritual strength and support you can obtain."

Fr. John looked into Argo's eyes as he reached across the table and clasped his hand firmly.

"I will pray for you to have that strength and wisdom, and I urge you to do the same. Call me immediately after the next contact."

He stood up from the table and left the restaurant. Argo finished his tea then walked out and hailed a cab.

Catherine

CATHERINE WAS ARGO'S FAVORITE CLIENT. Thirtyish, possessing a wholesome beauty of which she seemed hardly aware, a strong personality and warm nature, smart, well educated, ambitious, and full of energy. She was an attorney and worked in civil litigation. She had a full caseload at the law firm that employed her, but always had a handful of indigent clients that she handled on the outside. She worked on their behalf out of a sense of justice and a tendency toward altruism. Catherine had moved to New York after college to attend law school, and had been here ever since. She was originally from Cincinnati, where her parents now lived. Catherine had first come to see Argo five months ago, and began their introductory session with the statement: "I don't have a life, can you help me?"

Argo's saw his work with Catherine as assisting in transitioning the context of her life from high performing adolescent to self-actualizing, adult woman. There was no lurking psychosis or deep neurosis. She had reached a level of success and accomplishment which called for a shift in her outlook away from a childlike approval seeking to that of an adult living out of chosen values. He helped Catherine become aware of the invisible reins that had guided her thus far, assisting her in knowing her strengths and weaknesses, and choosing the values that would guide her choices in the future.

Her transference to Argo was both parental and romantic. It is very common for clients to have a 'crush' on their therapist, and clearly Catherine had those feelings for Argo. She vacillated between seeing him as a father and as a lover. Argo's countertransference to Catherine was symmetrical with hers. He had a concern for her like she was one of his daughters, and also felt a strong physical and romantic attraction to her. She tended to look in his eyes as they conversed, and he sometimes would look away when the warmth of her gaze became unbearable. He channeled this latent libidinous energy back into their work, using its power to add vitality to the therapy. Argo had begun his career in psychoanalysis in his forties, and sometimes wondered if he'd have been able to treat a woman as lovely as Catherine when he was younger and less self-aware. Crossing the line to sexual involvement with a client was unthinkable. It instantly destroyed the special relationship and eliminated the possibility of any further contribution. He cared deeply for the people he worked with, particularly this one. He knew he would never do anything to harm her.

Argo listened intently as she spoke. "My father asked me again to come home to help with mom, and I tried to explain that I can't. He doesn't understand, or he is too upset or too scared to hear what I'm saying. I've got a job to do here, and it just isn't a good time. I promised him I'd fly home at the end of the month for a weekend, but that was all

I could do right now. I'm handling a full caseload for the firm, and my pro-bono clients will have no one to look after them if I up and leave!"

Argo could see that Catherine was more hooked by what she felt were demands upon her than critical situations that needed immediate attention. He intervened to give her some perspective. "How is the housekeeper you hired for your parents working out?" he asked.

Catherine replied: "She is keeping the place clean, doing the shopping, and preparing dinner for Dad when he gets home each night."

"And the visiting nurse you arranged for?" He asked.

"She comes in three times a week, checks Mom's vitals, and bathes her. That seems to be under control." Catherine replied.

Argo could feel the conflict in her speaking. Catherine's mother had suffered a stroke two months ago. She was partially paralyzed, needed a lot of care and her father was handling it very poorly. Until the stroke had incapacitated Catherine's mother, her parents had had a very compartmentalized relationship. Her father had earned the money, and his wife had taken care of all matters relating to their home. Catherine's father had no idea how to cook, clean, do laundry, shop or any of the myriad other responsibilities of the household. He was lost and wanted his daughter home as much to take care of him as to look after her mother. Catherine had always tried to please her father, and was very upset that she could not satisfy his demands.

She continued. "Carl says it has made me moody. I know he wants to be supportive, but he says it's affecting our relationship. When I told him about going out there, he reminded me we had tickets to Forrest Hills that weekend. He's been acting more and more distant in the last several weeks and I'm afraid he may be thinking that it would be easier to 'move on'."

Catherine had related enough conversations with her boyfriend Carl for Argo to conclude that he was rather self-centered, immature and narcissistic. He decided to intervene at this point with a summary reflection that would help Catherine frame her situation with some context.

"You have your hands full. You are representing a dozen clients in separate legal proceedings, trying to manage your parent's household remotely from 800 miles away, while keeping your boyfriend happy. You haven't been to the gym in a month, or had a good night's sleep in weeks. You are doing everything you can, yet you have a sense that you are letting down the people close to you."

Catherine sounded desperate: "Nobody is happy with me."

Argo asked: "Do you remember what brought you to see me those many months ago?"

Catherine reflected for a few seconds, then blurted out:

"Of course, I didn't have a life, I was running around like a maniac trying to please everyone, but this is different!"

Argo kept probing: "Say more."

She thought for a moment, then replied.

"It isn't different really. The particular circumstances may be, but not the general ones. My response has been to revert to my 'good little girl' role."

Argo had a firm conviction that humor was one of the most effective tools for gaining perspective. He held her gaze silently, and allowed a slight smile to cross his face. Slowly Catherine's look of helplessness gave way and she started to laugh. She reached into her handbag, and after a moment of rummaging, pulled out a folded note.

"I saved it. Maybe I should tie it to my wrist!"

She held it up so he could see. Argo had passed it to her during a session several months ago, telling her it was a note from God. It read:

Dear Catherine,

Take the day off, I'll handle everything for the next 24 hours.

With Love,

God

They both laughed. The stress in her demeanor lightened visibly, and Argo was once again struck by her vibrant loveliness. Her hair was a deep auburn that had a magical translucence. It wasn't curly, but wasn't straight either; it fell perfectly around her face.

As Catherine leaned forward to put the note back, the opening at the collar of her blouse parted to briefly reveal the fullness of her breasts. Argo caught his breath; he was transfixed by her voluptuousness. She looked up suddenly and saw the longing wonder in his eyes. Argo raised his gaze to meet hers as he mentally kicked himself for being so careless. Authenticity is a key ingredient in the therapeutic relationship, and Argo was not sure how to play this out.

Catherine leaned forward, her eyes sought his.

"Dr. Masters, I look forward to seeing you each week more than anything else I do. I have never in my life been able to speak with someone who understood me and cared about me. You listen to me as if everything I say is gold. Do you know how important you are to me?"

Argo had his hands full now. His carelessness had activated the latent attraction between them and Catherine was exploring it. Her boldness in doing so was a tribute to what she had accomplished so far, but Argo felt off balance. What was worse, much worse, was a sudden awareness of his own ambivalence. Argo had been fooling himself about this - his desire to make love to this woman was stunningly powerful. Was it possible that they could be lovers...?

Catherine rose from her seat, crossed the room and knelt in front of Argo. She took his hands in hers and continued: "It isn't just the work we've done. We love the same things; that picture of you there on the wall hiking in the Rockies; in the last week I've dreamt of you and me doing that." Her face turned crimson as she realized what she had said.

Argo ran the fingers of his right hand through Catherine's hair and leaned toward her as he gazed into her eyes; the openness he saw there made him feel as if he were falling off a magical cliff into a heavenly chasm. He tilted his head to one side, and gazed as if in a trance into her eyes. Something stopped him; he felt tears beginning to brim in his eyes.

"Catherine, our sessions have been that way for me also. As we have become more acquainted, it has been impossible to repress a strong affection and affinity. I have loved the way you have worked hard. I have watched you blossom and grow. I have seen you face every sort of issue with courage. You have made the work we do a pleasure for me. Now we have come to an unexpected fork in the road. I saw it but failed to appreciate its power."

A look of alarm came across Catherine's face, and she interrupted: "Whatever the fork in the road is, I'm sure we can navigate it." She had raised her hands to his face and he felt the fingers of her right hand gently nudging the back of his neck as her voice trailed off.

The fragrance of her hair filled his nostrils; he felt intoxicated by her and wanted nothing other than to take her in his arms. He had no idea where he got the strength to push the desire down, but he remained in his chair, and continued: "You and I, Catherine, have traveled together along a rich road of emotional and psychic growth and exploration. The issue we must deal with now is how to proceed from here. There are two roads to choose from; one advances toward self-realization, the other toward chaos."

Argo struggled to choose his words carefully. As her therapist he knew she trusted him completely, and he was determined, that notwithstanding the overwhelming desire now confronting him, he would continue to honor what he considered his sacred commitment to act on her behalf.

"Catherine, Catherine, Catherine" he repeated.

Her eyes were wide and fawn-like in their vulnerability.

"There is only one acceptable role for me to take in our relationship, and that is to continue to walk beside you as a guide and mentor. The moment I step outside of the boundaries of the covenant I made as your therapist, the power of our relationship vanishes. I become a taker, and you become my victim. I will never let that happen. Do you understand what I am saying?" Argo felt a tear roll down his left cheek.

Catherine had often amazed Argo with her resilience, and he could see her taking possession of herself. She took his hands in hers and looked into his eyes.

"I trust you with my life, and intend to keep you in my life."

Argo lifted his hands to her temples, and kissed her forehead softly.

"Thank you Catherine." As he stood, he helped her to her feet.

"This is all for tonight. What we experienced this evening took us by surprise, but our alliance is intact – it's more than intact. Just keep doing what you've been doing, and trust yourself. I'll see you next week."

He walked her to the door that led to the waiting room and opened it. There, sitting quietly in the waiting room was Praggles. Catherine didn't seem to notice him as she exited to the hallway and turned with a small wave of farewell.

The Contract

PRAGGLES ROSE FROM HIS SEAT and stood peering at Argo. When the door to the hallway closed behind Catherine, he spoke.

"You could have easily seduced her. You didn't but you will always think about it, sometimes you will have difficulty thinking of anything else."

Argo remembered the third item in the note Praggles had handed him at the end of their first session, and its reference to his having to 'think again'. He had not connected the dots then, but now it was clear that Praggles had referred to his relationship with Catherine. Clients frequently test their therapists and it occurred to Argo that Praggles was right on schedule.

"If I had seduced her, I wouldn't be much of a therapist. Come in." He motioned for him to enter.

Praggles sat where he had the week before. His appearance was the same as the first meeting; well-cut black suit, immaculately groomed, alert, analytical, and palpably cold. As Argo monitored his responses to Praggles, he felt a chilling emotional aura. There was an unsettling, quality to Praggles' attentiveness, like having a crowd pressing in.

Argo began:

"I don't know who you are, but I am certain that you are not a psychotic. Even if I were to accept your claims about yourself at face value, the domains you inhabit are unknown; they may even be unknowable by me. I am motivated to work with you for several reasons, the chief among them is a personal fascination with what you are trying to accomplish. Right behind that is a sense that you are genuinely reaching out. However, there are issues we need to flatten before I can agree to do this. If we can resolve them, then we will create a therapeutic contract for the work we plan to do."

Praggles had listened intently, and now nodded in the affirmative. "Let's discuss your issues, Dr. Masters." he said with a wry smile.

Argo felt he was going out on the skinny branches. If he was wrong and Praggles was a psychotic, he would feel like a fool. On the other hand, he had never let that consideration stop him before. Argo proceeded:

"In the scriptures of most of the world's religions, Satan is understood to be the source of all evil. My own early religious training was full of warnings about not falling into Satan's hands. Every time somebody had the urge to do something wrong, the temptation to do so was attributed to Satan. Do you follow me so far?"

Praggles had listened to Argo with his head cocked to one side, and a small frown appeared on his face.

"Yes, I understand that all evil in the world is attributed to me, and that I am viewed as the source of all of it. Please get to the point."

Argo continued.

"I am a therapist. It is my intention that my work empowers people to live their lives in a fulfilling manner. It is widely understood that a fulfilled life is one integrated into the community of one's fellows, one that contributes to the well-being of human society and the planet as a whole. The issue is quite simple. You have said that you have become less effective at your work, as a result of unexpected competition. You seek my assistance in dealing with this issue. How can I assist you in regaining traction and effectiveness in your work, when that work is antithetical to human well-being?"

Praggles stared at him for a moment; Argo could feel a surge of potent psychic energy emanating from him. It was the emotional equivalent to being a passenger in a car speeding down a very bumpy road. Praggles' eyes appeared as a pupilless kaleidoscope, and for an instant his voice seemed to emanate from a closed mouth.

"Dr. Masters, please excuse my reticence, I am not accustomed to being interrogated."

He paused for a few seconds and when he resumed his mouth again moved in unison with his words.

"On the contrary, I think you will find that humanities' well-being hinges on my actions! What you have said is half correct. It is wrong to say I am the source of evil in the world. I am never the source of evil, although, as part of my function I may facilitate its expression. It is however correct to identify me as a source of temptation to evil. Would you like me to explain that?"

Argo was fascinated by a certain authority in Praggles' voice, and by the assertions he was making. He urged Praggles to continue.

"I would. Please explain about not being the author of evil, yet being a facilitator of its expression."

Praggles replied.

"Very well. Remember our discussion about spiritual beings? The part about each spirit having a function?"

"Yes. I remember."

Praggles continued.

"My function is to challenge each human being in such a way that they succeed or fail. These challenges occur in the domain of the unique, God-like gift each human being has been given – freedom to choose. What I will say now is an oversimplification, but will help you. Let us begin with the assertion that good people are not born - they are made. Can you understand that?"

Argo nodded and Praggles resumed.

"What constitutes a good person is one who, when tested, ultimately becomes stronger by solving the problems created by the temptation. A good person may be tested and fail, but will always come back to try again. A good person never stops seeking to overcome their failures. Every human being fails, but the good ones come back from their failures. It is the people who fail and then embrace their failure who become the authors of evil in the world. They go on to commit evil acts of their own free will. They start down a path of destruction from which most never return, and the destruction they create touches everyone around them."

Praggles stopped and peered at Argo.

"Please say more."

Praggles answer was immediate, it startled Argo how rapidly his intelligence worked.

"For reasons you do not now appreciate, it is impossible to provide the complete answer to your question. Don't be offended, but you do not possess the capacity to fully understand the answer. I will give you a conceptual view by referring to a scripture from the Christian tradition with which you are familiar, but have never understood. It illustrates the particular essence of goodness to which I refer. In this scripture a very wealthy and powerful man leaves three of his stewards in charge of his affairs whilst he travels abroad. The stewards have each been given a sum of money with which to conduct their master's business, and have complete freedom to do as they see fit. The master is away for many years. No one knows when he will return, but one day he does. He then calls each of the stewards to him and asks what they have done with the wealth entrusted to them.

The first replies that he has invested the resources of which he had charge and realized a substantial profit. The master's wealth has been multiplied by a factor. The master is very pleased, and rewards the steward with additional power and responsibility.

The master then interviews the second steward, who has also used the master's wealth in endeavors that have resulted in a modest profit. He informs his master that he has doubled the resources in his charge. The master tells this steward he has done well, and that he will continue to have charge of the resources he has been given.

The third steward is then questioned. This steward tells the master that he has done nothing with the resources he controlled, fearing that he would be punished if he failed or did not produce a profit. The master is outraged and casts this steward out of his household forever. Do you now begin to get a sense of what this scripture means?"

Argo remembered it, but was still puzzled by it.

"It is not clear to me. I think you are pointing to something central to the issues we need to resolve, and I'd like you to flesh it out for me. Can you do that?"

Praggles continued.

"It is an analogy for the relationship of the creator to humanity. Human kind is created with both spiritual and physical being. Unlike any other beings, humans have been granted the power to make choices. At the point a human being begins to exercise freedom of choice, I intervene to show them the dark side. The sum and substance of a human life is the net of the choices they have made - how they used the resources they were given."

Argo was struggling.

"It is difficult for me to understand how that works. Let's contrast the life of person born to wealth and privilege in a stable country and the life of an orphan in Somalia. How is judgment possible?"

Praggles again responded without hesitation.

"The question is the same; each has the freedom to choose how they use their lives within the environment around them. No two people have the same gifts, but each person, no matter what their status, has the freedom to employ what they have or not."

Praggles scanned Argo's face.

"Why is this so difficult for you to understand?"

Argo was enthralled by what Praggles was saying, and he wasn't going to stop teasing it out until he was certain.

"I am thinking specifically about an eight year old child who was playing in the street and was killed in a drive by shooting last night in the South Bronx. What was her freedom of choice?"

"Your question highlights the lack of discernment most of you possess about these events. The dead child was killed by one of your kind. The person who killed the girl is someone I interacted with once, many years ago. I presented him with an alternative. He was thirteen years old, and his mother and father, fearing that he would be influenced to join one of the local gangs, had arranged for him to reside with relatives living in the rural South. I suggested to him that he did not have to go. He chose to run away from home, so he could stay with his friends. I have not had any interactions with him since. It has not been necessary."

"Please say more about it not being necessary."

"His choice then, and almost all the choices he has made since are consistent; he has chosen a direction for his life. If he began to contemplate a different life, one more in line with his gifts, then it might be necessary for me to test him further, but he hasn't."

Argo: "What about the dead girl?"

Praggles: "The death of the child is a consequence of choices made by the young man. Choice always entails consequences. The only way to avoid them is to remove the gift."

Argo pressed further.

"Is the girl's death a neutral event for you?"

Praggles response was cold and precise.

"Killing is rarely in my interest, it reduces the pool of humanity with whom I can work."

"Are you saying that murder and mayhem are not your doing?"

Praggles response was blunt.

"Yes. That is rarely my intent."

Argo's mind was racing. Praggles was painting a picture of Satan that had never occurred to him. He summarized what he'd heard as much to clarify it for himself as to let Praggles know he had heard him.

"You seem to be saying that what makes a human being strong spiritually and morally is the work they do when they are tempted, and that you are the author of that temptation. The successful human being either resists the temptation, or if not, works to regain what they lost as a result of failing. Either way they become stronger through the exercise of working to do what they know is right. Those who do not resist, but embrace the temptation, do not become strong, because they have done no work to perfect themselves. Is that accurate?"

Praggles nodded.

"It is essentially correct. My temptations are designed to offer human beings the full spectrum of choices by presenting the ones that appeal to their dark side."

Argo responded.

"It would be helpful if you used an example. Can you think of one that might expand my understanding?"

Praggles sat motionless for a moment; his face an empty mask. When he began to speak, there was a change in his voice and demeanor that suggested he was completely absorbed.

"I will give you an extraordinary example; one who illustrates a complete surrender to evil – Adolf Hitler. Would he be suitable?"

Argo was sure Praggles knew of his effort to understand the roots of the immeasurable suffering Hitler created. He leaned forward nodding.

Praggles began.

"Adolf Hitler came from humble beginnings, yet it was clear that he possessed an extraordinary ability to influence people. It was his gift. He was foreordained to become a great leader. From an early age he had a tendency to resentment; he did not resist this tendency. I had one and only one interaction with him, which occurred when he was twenty years old. He was very politically aware, and had been exposed to the hoax your historians have named 'The Protocols of the Elders of Zion'. I tempted him to hate the Jews. He made a choice to embrace this hatred. At first he saw it as a political issue to be exploited, but he dwelled on it and nurtured it until it became the central theme of his life and leadership. Everything he did after embracing that hatred, he created on his own. The objects of his hatred multiplied to many others. He carried it to lengths that sent shudders of horror even through spiritual domains. He did so without any help from anyone. Once he turned his face toward evil, he never looked back. Aside from the one conversation I had with him, neither my minions nor I ever interacted with him again."

Argo wondered how Praggles saw his part in what had occurred.

"Do you see yourself as having any responsibility for the result?"

Praggles leaned forward like a prizefighter who sees an opening.

"When you were in the fourteenth year of life, I tempted you to despise your parents. You embraced the temptation and your relationship with them was never the same. Am I responsible for the choice you made?"

Suddenly Argo's memory of the choice was as vivid as the day he had made it; the unending spiral of disappointments that had convinced him his mother and father had no business being his parents flooded his mind. He had to use every molecule of his will to remain composed. He was angered by what Praggles had said, and his reply reflected that.

"I made that choice, however I will say that you presented the possibility of it at my weakest moment."

Praggles again countered without hesitation.

"Weakest? You were becoming more ready to make that choice every day. You were guilty of the most primary existential mistake - believing that what is should not be. It is the most prolific source of human suffering. You hated your life and believed you were entitled to a better one. I tempted you to blame your parents, and you did. Every choice you made after that was on your own. You followed the dark road of blame and resentment. Your actions harmed you and every member of your family. It led to the brink of your own destruction. What distinguishes you is that there was a part of you that never accepted the choice you made, and one day you became willing to re-evaluate the course you had set for your life."

Praggles peered at him like a prosecutor.

"Would it be accurate to say that it is the work you have done to recover from that choice and rebuild your life that has made you who you are today?"

Argo could see the truth of what Praggles described clearly. The temptation had defined the arena in which he would be perfected or destroyed. Argo had made the choice without compulsion. He had struggled for 23 years and come within a hairsbreadth of being annihilated by alcoholism before turning from the terrible path upon which he had so readily embarked. Although he felt overwhelmed, he knew Praggles was giving him the information he needed to make the choice confronting him now. He wondered if Praggles knew what he was thinking before he spoke:

"I concur with your assessment that the work I have done has had the effect of perfecting me. I have several other areas of concern."

Praggles indicated that Argo should proceed with a small motion of his right hand. Argo sat straight up and looked directly into Praggles eyes as he began:

"You have already stated several times that you understand that our communications must be direct and without subterfuge if they are to be useful. Your conversations with me so far have demonstrated that. In order for us to work together effectively you must continue to communicate with me in this manner."

Praggles nodded.

"It would be pointless to do otherwise. You also have another request which you are not sure how to state concerning harm to yourself and others."

At first Argo had been uncomfortable that Praggles could read his thoughts, but he had already determined that his ability to do so was inconsistent. He needed to understand the limits of his client's clairvoyance.

"I want your promise that no harm will come to me or the people I am connected to as a result of our working together."

Praggles' response was consistent with what he had said earlier.

"I have a job to do, and I will continue to do it. I will not do it any differently because of the work we do. There is no circumstance where I will alter my actions toward any individual because of the work we do. The experience you had with your client Catherine tonight should make that clear to you. You have another question."

Argo had been holding back on asking the question that most troubled him. He almost winced as he asked.

"Will I offend the Creator if I choose to work with you?"

Praggles spoke slowly and thoughtfully as he replied.

"I do not know what you ask with certainty. There is no communication –the Creator does not guide my work. I am able to see the level of connection each human being has to the Creator, and have seen that you have developed a keen sensitivity in that arena. If the Creator did not want you to do this, you would know."

Clearly Praggles had left it up to him to make the determination. He silently recited the Serenity Prayer that had been a staple of his sobriety, and knew he had never meant it more than now. He sat up in his chair, flipped to a new page on his pad, turned to Praggles.

"Let's go to work."

Praggles nodded, and Argo continued.

"You have spoken about another source of temptation; one that rivals your own and interferes with your ability to do your intended work. Please tell me about that."

When he spoke, Praggles features seemed sharper and his voice ceased to convey the same authority it had a moment before.

"People access that which is spiritual in a state of solitude – it is in that domain that thought and reflection can connect with the resources and pitfalls of the spiritual universe. It is there that human beings exercise their freedom to make the choices that shape them and their lives. Solitude is where the Creator's voice can be heard; it is also the domain in which they will have their conversations with me. A number of forces and circumstances are combining that make solitude unavailable. There are a growing number of human beings that never experience it. Technology has been developed by human kind that now enables people to completely avoid that state. A growing number of people are plugged into electronic media of some sort every waking moment of every day. When they are not being bombarded with information streams that fully occupy them, they are initiating their own by communicating with others - even with people half a world away. Walk down any busy street and notice how many people are on their cell phones, typing on their Blackberrys, playing portable video games, surfing the Internet, listening to music or even watching television. Many people now grow up without ever having experienced being alone with themselves. These people are crippled."

Argo offered a clarifying intervention.

"When you spoke of competition, I thought you were referring to some alternate temptation, but this sounds like a shift in the environment. Where is the competition?"

Praggles responded immediately.

"Don't you see? It is the Peter Pan temptation to remain as one is, to never advance, to live without having chosen values, to assume a mass consciousness. Human beings are born innocent and in the intended scheme of life, lose that innocence meeting the trials embedded in their environment and dealing with the temptations I give them. Today's plugged in human beings go from innocence to a state of undistinguished consciousness in which they are constantly occupied and titillated by the media streams in which they are immersed. They have to deal with the tactical challenges of their environment, but never venture into the spiritual domain, never experience solitude and what is possible there. The result is spiritual atrophy. They have no values, no noble missions, and no grand schemes. They limit their choices to selecting media streams that will provide the best entertainment and stimulation. They meet in electronic forums to exchange information about where to access the best pornography, latest video games, music downloads, sports editorials, and whom to date. Ethics and morality and the struggles to identify and resolve issues pertaining to it are considered archaic, a bore, a thing to be avoided."

Argo interjected with a question hoping to get clarity on something that was gnawing at him.

"And this is a problem for you why?"

Praggles closed his eyes and said nothing for a moment. When he began there was a trace of something like weariness in his voice.

"Dr. Masters please understand that our conversation, however difficult for you, is quite challenging to me also. My choice to speak with you is unprecedented. I have never had a conversation with a human being before that did not involve temptation or subterfuge. We must communicate in a manner that is mutually clear if anything is to be accomplished. Please know that I am working very hard to do that. I will attempt to answer your question, even though it is something you should have been able to deduce."

Argo was not accustomed to his clients thinking of him as dense, and knew he could have executed his last intervention more skillfully. He encouraged Praggles to continue.

"I appreciate your patience, please bear with me. I am trying to fully understand what you are saying and must be sure not to insert my own assumptions. At some level, it would seem that diverting human beings from ever examining the real issues of life would save you the trouble of having to tempt them in the first place."

Praggles responded.

"The circumstances I have described are a problem for a number of reasons. As you will recall the purpose for which I was created is to tempt human beings at strategic points in their lives so that they can choose to realize their strengths or submit to their weaknesses. These people are not even on the playing field. I cannot fulfill this purpose any longer for a significant portion of humanity."

Argo interjected with a question.

"Are these media streams destructive even to mature, intelligent and morally stable people? Are they destructive to everyone?"

Praggles considered the question and replied.

"Let me begin by giving you some context by contrasting my attentional capabilities with your own. My attention range is unlimited; I can attend to an infinite number of things simultaneously. As you and I speak, I also fulfill my intended functions by monitoring every living human being. Can you understand that?"

Argo had read theological accounts of the infinite mind, but its import had not hit home till now.

"You are telling me that as we speak, you are also attending to the rest of the human race?"

"That is correct. Do you know the attention range of the average human being?"

Argo replied:

"My recollection of results of cognitive studies done in the last two decades are that the maximum number of symbols the human working memory can manipulate at any one time is limited to 7 or 8 items. This can be increased slightly by grouping similar symbols into categories then using the categories, but the total number is still very finite."

Praggles continued.

"The human mind is much more nimble in the spiritual domain than the logical domain. In the domain of logical thinking, the number of variables a human being can attend to at any one time is quite small. When the media streams completely occupy their capacity, nothing else can get in. Your political scientists have created the term 'strategic misdirection'. Have you heard of it?"

"Yes. If you present a person with enough diverse information, they tend to lose the ability to distinguish which items are important and which are meaningless."

Praggles nodded.

"What is happening is much like that. The proliferation of devices for instantly gratifying the desire to obtain information and be in communication with others has spawned endless media streams for sports scores, dating, mating, video games, chat rooms, pornography, televised programs of every kind, shopping, gambling – it is endless. Every waking moment of every day is filled with this. Further, the organizations that control this media employ sophisticated techniques to measure then improve the penetration of their products. They track the interests of each customer and potential customer via automated data collection procedures that monitor internet, cell phone and credit card usage, then target them with individually tailored marketing products. It is very effective, and it is everywhere."

As Praggles has spoken his voice and demeanor had grown more intense to the point where Argo could barely tolerate it. He continued to press him to refine the problem definition.

"Your description of the competition is breathtaking. It is so present, so everywhere, that I have become accustomed to it. Clearly there is a primary difference between your temptation and the marketing of the vendors of these products. How would you characterize it?"

Praggles did not hesitate.

"The intent and purpose of my temptations are to test human beings in a way that will either destroy or develop them; they are finite. The competition's marketing is motivated solely by a desire for profits and power. It is like a fire that spreads more quickly as it gets bigger. It does not develop human beings; it chokes their intellects with noise, until it is impossible for them to hear the things that would allow them to participate in a spiritual life."

In that moment Argo knew he had established a therapeutic connection with Praggles; there was a subtle change in his speaking, as if finally sharing this information had begun to enable him to process it too. Praggles looked at him and held up a hand.

"Dr. Masters, it is time for me to go. Our session has taken its toll on you."

Argo knew Praggles was right, but Praggles' promise to provide insights and information about spiritual matters trumped his desire for rest. He did not want to wait for the answer to a question that had been gnawing at him. He held up his hand to signal his desire to speak.

"Before you go, I have a question. Do you mind?"

Praggles rose from his seat as if readying to leave, and said.

"You would like me to explain a phenomenon which puzzles you, namely a growing tendency among educated human beings to believe that science has transcended the need for God. The credo goes something like this: science and technology are rapidly working toward solutions to all the major issues facing humanity. You don't share that belief, but are alarmed at the inability of your fellows to see what you see. Sometimes you wonder if it is you, and not them, who is misguided. Is that accurate?"

Argo nodded and waited.

Praggles seemed to mull it over for a moment, then began.

"Very well, but I must tell you that you may not possess the ability to understand the answer, however it pleases me to share them with you."

Praggles remained standing, now facing Argo squarely. He began.

"Imagine an ant that lived near the edge of a sidewalk, and often saw human beings walk past. Now make an estimate of how much information and understanding of human beings the ant would have absorbed from that experience. What knowledge of human beings do you think the ant possesses?"

Argo had no ambivalence.

"None. The experience would be beyond the capabilities of the ant to interpret."

Praggles nodded as if to agree.

"The ants live in a lower cosmos than human beings; they understand the laws that govern that cosmos. Their cosmos is lower down the scale than the cosmos in which humanity resides. You can see your own cosmos and can also look into those cosmos lower down in the hierarchy, such as that of the ants and insects. They however cannot look up the hierarchy to see you. The ants are affected by the events in your cosmos, but cannot understand or influence those events. If humans build a house and dig up the domain of the ants, that is that.

Yet that is the same situation in which human beings find themselves. The cosmos of the creator is at the top of the hierarchy of cosmos; you are subject to its laws and the laws of the intervening cosmos, as well as the laws of your own cosmos. You cannot see into that cosmos. The qualities and characteristics of the Creator are not directly visible to you. Most of you do not understand this limitation, and misinterpret your inability to access the Creator's cosmos as evidence of nonexistence. Human beings have been endowed with an ability to attain limited glimpses of the Creator's manifestations, but only by rigorous spiritual work. Very few do that work anymore; preferring to rely on your so called science.

Further, most of you fail to understand the work of your scientists, and grossly inflate the nature of scientific accomplishments. Would you be shocked to learn that if every scientist and engineer on the face the earth were brought together in one place and tasked with creating even one blade of grass from scratch, they could not do it? Few understand this. They have misinterpreted reports of the work scientist have done with DNA to include creating life. Scientists have never created any form of life. All the cloning, all the gene splicing is nothing more than ingenious mechanical alterations performed on pre-existing organic mater. How is it that one cell in even the most complex organism, something microscopically small, can contain all the information needed to reproduce the entire organism? How is it that even the simplest green plant employs the process of photosynthesis, yet your science cannot duplicate or explain that ubiquitous process? The problem is exacerbated by the pervasive distractions we discussed earlier that increasingly obscure even simple realities. The divine mystery of creation has been declared to be no mystery at all. Divine Creation has been dismissed on the assumption that life was brought about by accident or random chance. The number of events and conditions that would have to occur to create even a simple one celled creature capable of nourishing and reproducing itself are even now beyond humanity's power to enumerate or duplicate. Yet the effects of the acceptance of this fiction are a complete devaluation of all things created. If all life occurs as a result of a cosmic accident, then nothing really matters. It is now possible for people to live their entire lives so embedded in meaningless noise that they are completely oblivious to the profound forces that created and surround them. That is the short version of my opinion. I hope it helps you."

Praggles walked toward the door.

Argo tried to rise, but Praggles gestured for him stay seated.

"I'll let myself out. Until next week."

He stopped and seemed to hesitate as if pondering something; then a cold sneer appeared on his face.

"Please give my regards to your friend, Fr. John. Tell him I said hello, and that his daughter is doing well. By the way, if you want to understand more about the ants and the cosmoses, he will be able to assist you."

Before Argo could respond Praggles was gone.

Argo was struggling between surrendering to a profound sense of weariness, and the gaggle of questions that clamored into his consciousness. He wrote the following on a fresh page in Praggles' file:

-Client appears angered by mankind's taking credit for the works of God, yet he is the author of that behavior. What does this mean?

-What did his remarks about Fr. John mean?

-Which of my thoughts can't he access?

He then called Fr. John's mobile number. The priest answered immediately.

"He was here on schedule. Either he is who he says, or I'm losing my mind. As it was with the first visit, I am utterly exhausted and my first priority is to get some rest. Can we talk tomorrow?"

The priest understood, and asked for a call in the morning when Argo awakened.

Argo was too tired to go home. He put the file away, opened the bottom drawer of his desk, pulled out a small blanket, went to the couch, took his shoes off, lay down and pulled the blanket over himself. He put a small throw pillow under his head and was asleep as his eyes closed.

Supervision

ARGO CALLED FR. JOHN the next morning. He reached the parish house, and recognized the brogue of the woman answering the phone. She offered to take a message, but when he told her his name, she asked him to hold the line. A moment later the priest's voice greeted him.

"I've been waiting for your call. When can we meet and discuss how the session went?"

Argo had not realized how badly he needed to speak to the priest.

"I am very, very glad to hear your voice. I'll let you decide how the session went after you hear the details."

Maddeningly, the priest's various parish duties and Argo's patient schedule synched badly preventing a meeting till evening. They arranged to meet at 7PM at a pub at 44th St and 10th Ave. They would have dinner and discuss the session.

Argo arrived just at 7. The pub's bar was doing a brisk trade with what looked like the after-work crowd. As Argo moved toward the back many of the faces he passed were illuminated by the glow of the cell phones into which they gazed. He spotted Fr. John half standing in his seat in a booth at the far corner, waving. He took his coat off as he made his way back, then settled in opposite the priest. Fr. John's voice reflected the concern on his face.

"You don't look well Argo."

"John, it has been a long couple of days. Thank you again for being my anchor to reality, I couldn't fly solo on this. How about we order before we get started, so we won't be interrupted? I've got a lot to tell you."

Once the waitress had taken the order, Argo began.

"Either I am losing my mind or Praggles is who he claims to be."

Fr. John's brow wrinkled.

"If you are right, that is very bad news. Tell me everything you can."

Argo took a deep breath as he decided where to start.

"There is nothing about him to suggest psychosis. Just as in the first visit his sense of time and place was exact, his appearance impeccable, and his ability to understand and deliver the most nuanced communications was spot on. I am no longer convinced that his claim about his identity are delusional.

Two of the satanic qualities you mentioned in our first meeting were an inability to experience love, and a hatred for mankind. Both those qualities were present. There was not a hint of attachment in anything he said, and ample evidence of a jealous resentment of all humanity. He possesses knowledge and abilities that are outside the range of what we know to be human.

As he was leaving he turned and asked me to convey a message to you".

Fr. John's expression morphed from concern to surprise.

"Oh? What did he say exactly?"

Argo repeated the message verbatim. The priest caught his breath and his face reddened.

"Well, well, well, how considerate of Mr. Praggles to reach out to me. I'll fill you in on what that meant once you've finished. Let me digest it first. Why don't we go through the events of the session? Tell me everything you can remember from start to finish."

Argo began by relating what had occurred in Catherine's session, and how his sexual countertransference to her had blown up in his face.

"I had never crossed the line with a patient, but Praggles predicted I would do just that in the third point of his letter. It got out of hand, but very briefly, and without doing irrevocable harm to the therapeutic relationship. When I escorted her out to the waiting room, there he was. He began his conversation with me by commenting that I could have seduced her. He knew that I hadn't. He clearly had knowledge of what went on between us."

Fr. John nodded.

"I have read of disclosures like this during exorcisms. Go on."

The food was served while Argo spoke, but both men were so engaged they ate sparingly - grabbing nibbles between sentences.

Argo told the priest about the discussions of Satan's functions, the claims Praggles made that they were essential to human spiritual development, and why he felt he could no longer fulfill his role. He reviewed the examples Praggles used, his reference to Argo's catastrophic choice to reject his parents, the use of scriptural sources, and the discourse on the inherent costs the gift of free choice entailed. He spoke of how Praggles presence exhausted him, and that Praggles had known it would. He related how Praggles seemed able to hear his thoughts, and would often respond as if Argo had spoken them.

Fr. John listened without interrupting; making occasional notes on a scrap of paper. When it was clear that Argo had finished, he spoke.

"Argo, my first concern is that you are ok. Just listening to your experience of this has my heart pounding. As you spoke I kept looking for the loophole; the thing that would explode Praggles' story into a comedic farce, but there is nothing here that has that ring. What is your mental state right now?"

"Thank you for your concern John. I can't adequately express how much it means to me. Praggles visits are like a window into another dimension, and I have felt psychically off balance since first seeing him. I was afraid you would listen to what I said and then tell me I needed psychiatric help – that I'd become delusional. I am desperate for your feedback and support."

Argo's words had the ring of a plea. The priest reached over and patted his forearm.

"Argo, I am with you in this, where ever it leads.

Let me fill in one of the blanks for you and explain his remark as he left you. You know a lot about my past from sharing I did in AA meetings we both attended, but there is a part of my life about which I have never spoken. I became a priest after my first recovery from alcoholism, but I relapsed after being sober for fifteen years. At that time I had advanced to the rank of monsignor in the church, and had my own parish. I had an affair with a woman during the relapse. She became pregnant, and we have a daughter together. The child is what propelled me back into recovery. I chose to remain in the priesthood. The church demoted me to the status of parish priest, but that too seems to have been for the best. Her mother and I speak about what is best for our daughter, I pay support, but aside from the day she was born, I have never been with her. Her mother feels strongly that it would stigmatize her to know her father was a priest. I have never mentioned this outside the confessional, because it reflects badly on the Church. Do you have any questions about what I've told you?"

Argo had felt obsessed by his meeting with Praggles, yet the priest's disclosure and the obvious pain it caused him helped him regain perspective.

"The look on your face made it clear it had hit a nerve. If we're going to work together on this, we can't have any secrets from one another."

Fr. John nodded.

"I agree. After listening to each other in the AA meetings for a couple of years, I don't think either of us is shy about disclosing the personal stuff. Listen to me Argo - I am completely stunned by what you are telling me. There is not an atom of doubt in my mind that Praggles is satanic if not Satan. I just don't get it, why therapy? Do you have any thoughts about that?"

Argo shrugged.

"I am operating without knowing where this is going. That is almost always the case with new clients. It eventually plays out that everything that needs to be revealed to distinguish the direction for the work comes to the surface. What I am seeing so far with Praggles is unfolding like that. The hardest thing for me is maintaining detachment, and not getting hooked by my lifelong prejudices. His transference is both transparent and powerful, in fact it is so strong I fear it may overcome me if he really becomes enraged. I have to let him say what he has to say. I'm not a sound wall, I give feedback, but you know that clients work out much of what they need, simply by going through the exercise of articulating it. Praggles is doing the same; I can feel it. The weirdest thing is that I find myself regarding him the same way as my other clients - there is something that eludes him the illumination of which will be the key to understanding for him and us also. My fear is that with Praggles I'm not fulfilling my chosen role as a healer, but rather engaging in an act of colossal pride."

The priest seemed anxious to address this.

"Any motivation other than serving the Lord will result in catastrophe - it is a dangerous and tricky undertaking. Praggles came to you and made a compelling case for you to work with him. There are several glaring inconsistencies in his story, which I'll get to in a moment. One of the dangers I see for you and even for myself, is that working with Praggles may provide glimpses into things men have always wondered about, but never had access. It is heady stuff. Somehow we have to keep each other from losing perspective. Beyond that, this work is extremely dangerous, it could cost both of us our lives and our souls. Is that more clear now?"

Argo concurred.

"That is my fear also, yet for me there is a sense of being destined for this. It has been growing in me since the World Trade Center attacks. I have to do this, no matter how dangerous it is. I believe there will be an opportunity to do some real good, if I can last long enough. Can you understand that?"

The priest demeanor mirrored his words.

"I'm not sure. What is this 'good' that you think you'll do?"

Argo shook his head slowly.

"That is not clear to me yet – it is a gut feeling, a hunch really."

Argo returned to the subject of Praggles' visit.

"Speak to me about your concerns with Praggles' story."

The priest took a deep breath, and began.

"The most eloquent and complete description of Satan ever written is contained in John Milton's 'Paradise Lost'. It is an exhaustive account of his fall as well as his motivations. Are you familiar with it?"

Argo nodded.

"I am, but it has been a very long time since I read it. It seemed full of mythological references that were completely unfamiliar to me. I was a student fulfilling an assignment - the context is very different now."

A troubled expression seemed to flit across the priest's face.

"Those mythological references you speak of were once common knowledge to any educated person. Much of the knowledge the book was based on has 'vanished' from the mainstream. We live in a world today that has lost its connection with the wisdom of the past. But bear with me while I go over some high spots. First, Satan before the rebellion was named Lucifer, the angel of light. He was one of God's most glorious creations, and in rank second only to God. He was magnificent and admirable in every way, but over time became filled with pride. Worshipping the Creator became onerous for him; and eventually he sought to make himself equal to God. He led the first revolt. One of the claims he made was that neither he nor any of the other spiritual inhabitants of heaven had been created by God, and were therefore not beholden to God. He enrolled large numbers of the heavenly host to follow him. It resulted in his fall, as well as the fall of the multitudes that followed him. There was not a hint of repentance in Lucifer. From that point forward he became known as Satan. He and his followers were cast into the pit of hell to suffer forever. Satan's pride would not allow him to seek forgiveness; nor even admit to those that had followed him, that he had led them astray. Instead he adopted the role of the spoiler. He had been vanquished, but never surrendered. His twisted reasoning was he would claim equality with the Creator by destroying or perverting the works of the Creator. He had heard about the creation of earth and mankind from his followers, and found a way out of hell to investigate. It was then that he stumbled upon Adam and Eve in the Garden of Eden, and set about to destroy the Creator's masterpiece. He tempted Eve by suggesting that God had forbidden them to eat from the tree of knowledge to prevent them from becoming equal to him. Essentially a variation of the same ploy he had used to recruit those who followed him in the heavenly rebellion."

Argo remembered the story as the priest spoke.

"This points to a diametrically different motivation for his 'work', than the one he presented to me. He has either projected the responsibility of his actions back onto the creator, or he is outright lying. Some of his accusations about humanity were pure hypocrisy - they are behaviors he initiated. Taking credit for creation is the primary example. Today's widespread belief that all life has evolved from a simple organism that was created by random chance billions of years ago set the stage for the rejection of the idea of a divine origin. How people live their lives is profoundly influenced by whether they believe they exist as the result of a divine Creator's intention, or are simply here by random chance. Claiming that creation is a result of random chance may have come full circle - it certainly seems to be causing some of the issues that trouble Praggles. But, what he related that rang true for me was his statement that people either succumb to the temptations offered and run with them, or resist. Resistance produces strength of character. I intuitively gravitate to that notion."

The priest interrupted him.

"That view may have some validity, but completely ignores the abundant grace provided to each of us. I hope you see that."

Argo responded.

"I do see that. His visit has created as many questions as answers. I believe he has a hidden agenda in coming to me, but also that he has issues of which he is unaware. Uncovering those issues will provide the key."

The priest nodded.

"I agree that his purpose in seeking you out is completely obscured - perhaps even from him. Do you think it is either safe or sensible to continue?"

Argo feigned a thoughtful hesitation.

"Hmmm, perhaps I could ask buildings security to escort him out next time he shows up."

Fr. John did not seem amused.

"So there is no way to break this off?"

Argo shook his head.

"That is not possible any longer; I have agreed to work with him."

Argo was exhausted and suddenly longed to be home in bed.

"John, I have to get some rest, can we wrap up for now? Unless something changes, I will meet with him next Thursday evening. Please call me any time you have a thought, concern or suggestion prior to then, otherwise I'll call you after the session and we'll meet again next Friday evening. Is there anything else?"

"Yes - you have said that he seems able to read your thoughts. When you meet next - see if you can determine if that is always the case, or if he can only read certain types of thoughts."

"I have been exploring that, and I think there are limits to what he sees, but let me look into that more in our next session."

"Do - it may be important."

Argo could see that Fr. John was not finished.

"Just one more thing. How are you planning to proceed with your client Catherine?"

Argo shrugged.

"I'm not sure yet. Why?"

The priest did not reply immediately. It was clear he was uncomfortable.

"Argo, be very careful. You have feelings for this client. Are you sure that in continuing to treat her you are operating in her best interests, as well as your own?"

Argo's felt his face redden.

"John, I asked you to supervise my treatment of Praggles, not my entire practice. I'd like you to respect that boundary."

The priest sat back and regarded Argo quietly for a moment. In the silence Argo felt both embarrassment and regret for the sharpness of his reply. Presently the priest spoke.

"She is now within that boundary. This is no ordinary work we are undertaking. Any lapse in integrity, any weakness, may be leveraged by Praggles. If your motivation for continuing to treat her is based on anything but her best interests, you will put all three of us in danger. Don't imagine for a moment that Praggles wouldn't use her to manipulate you. We need to go further with this. I would like you to reflect on what we are doing here, and meet me at the parish house tomorrow. Can you do that?"

Argo checked his calendar.

"I am free from 3 to 5:30PM tomorrow - can we meet at 3:15?"

Fr. John nodded and offered Argo his hand; he grasped it in both of his. Argo valued the priest's wisdom and heart - he was a strong ally. The two men exited the pub together, and then walked in separate directions.

Unity

A good night's sleep had helped, but he still felt weary. Argo found the parish house; it was a narrow, but tidy brownstone adjacent to the church where he'd reconnected with the priest. Its entrance was at the top of a short stairway whose steps and railings were of the same limestone as the building's fascade. He rang the bell, and shortly a middle-aged housekeeper answered the door. He asked for Fr. John and she beckoned him to enter, then escorted him midway down an austere hallway and knocked upon a solid looking, black wooden door.

"Father - you've got a visitor."

Fr. John opened the door a moment later, thanked the woman and welcomed Argo.

"Well, you made it! May I get you some coffee or tea?"

Argo responded with a forced cheerfulness that he didn't feel.

"Absolutely yes, coffee with milk, but no sugar, please!"

He could see himself posturing, and realized how uncomfortable he was; there was a lurking defensiveness in his mood. He had a visceral dislike of situations where he might have to explain himself – he knew this, but it didn't make it easier.

Argo scanned the room – it was orderly and plain, devoid of warm accents, except for an ornately framed picture of a young girl on the desk. There was a brass crucifix over the entrance door.

The priest ushered Argo into his office; motioning for him to sit on the small sofa that occupied the back wall. He poured two cups of coffee from a pot that was brewing on small settee, and placed them on the table in front of the couch, then took a seat at the opposite end so that the two men faced each other obliquely.

"Argo, I'm very glad you are here and thank you for being open to having this discussion. The situation in which we are enmeshed, as it begins to open up, is taking on a nature and scope that is beyond anything I had imagined. How does it strike you?

Argo nodded.

"It is outside anything I ever dreamed of experiencing. I don't doubt that it's happening, but I feel very off balance."

The priest seemed to weigh Argo's response.

"Yes. Beings like Praggles exist in the shadows outside the realm of conscious experience, but there is nothing unconvincing about his presence. As that has sunk in for me, my perception of the nature of the task confronting us has changed. There is much more at stake, and the role we will have is becoming clearer.

I have spoken with my superior at the parish – Monsignor Dugan about this matter. He instructed me to report to the clergy responsible for such matters at the Archdiocese. They felt the matter significant enough to send it up the chain of command, where it has generated intense interest, and some skepticism. Evidently this encounter is unlike any previously recorded. The Church's direct experience with Satanic spirits is limited to those instances of demonic possession where the rite of exorcism is employed. As far as the Church is concerned, this is the first known instance of Satan initiating an overt contact for the purpose of communicating. He is reaching out specifically to you even though it is unclear what he wants. There is no doubt there is something very pressing on his mind - it is deemed vital that we discover what that is. You asked me to supervise your treatment of Praggles in order to maintain a proper therapeutic perspective. That will be insufficient; the role you are to play may go beyond what you can now imagine. Does what I'm saying surprise to you?"

Argo had replayed the prior evening's conversation with the priest in his head again and again. He had rebuffed the priest because did not want him interfering with his treatment of Catherine. That seemed petty now. He wondered if his change attitude was due to a growing sense of vulnerability. He needed the priest, but not the Roman Catholic Church. Argo decide to keep his reservations about the Church to himself. He had a hunch that Fr. John would not put the Church's interests before his own.

"I hear you, but feel profoundly clueless about what comes next. Before we tackle that let me say that I regret being short with you last night. After reflecting on what is occurring, I find myself feeling almost desperate - I am grateful for your steadiness and rectitude."

The priest gestured as if dismissing the need to even mention the interaction.

"Argo, you had just spent an hour with the most implacably evil being in creation, and evidently you will spend many more like it. If we agree that this situation is radically more significant and dangerous than originally thought, can you and I recalibrate our approach so that we have a good chance of handling it properly?"

Argo pushed aside his ambivalence. The priest was right - this thing was bigger than either of them had imagined, and they would have to work together, or fail.

"I'm convinced John. What are your thoughts about how best to proceed?"

"Argo, I'll begin by making an assertion that you may find offensive, but you may be sure I'm not trying to insult you. Are you ready?"

Argo was quite puzzled, but curious.

"Okay, John - fire away."

"Thank you Argo - you're a brave man! So here goes. I assert that you are not capable of working with Praggles. Make no mistake about what I mean - I believe you to be an excellent therapist, and a compassionate and moral man, but you are not up to the task of delivering therapy to Praggles."

Argo did not like what he was hearing, but wanted the priest to give him a better idea of what he meant.

"Will you tell me why you think that?"

"I will explain, but I want to be sure you know where I'm coming from - I am wholly on your side. I see this encounter differently than you do, and see vulnerabilities in you that may cause you to fail, and lead to a tragic end. I can and will help you overcome those if you let me. I'd like to speak of them now."

Argo was surprised by his reaction to these statements by the priest - he did not feel defensive. He wanted to know what the priest saw.

"I can't promise that I'll agree with your assessment, but my ears are wide open.

The priest was encouraged by Argo's openness - it was a good sign.

"You and I listen to people every day as they speak about their lives. Frequently they seem torn by conflicting needs.

They may try to be logical, but they also have emotional and physical drives and needs. One moment they are driven by one thing, and then their mood changes and they want something entirely different. It is like they are multiple people squeezed into one body."

Argo looked puzzled.

"John, I'm not following you."

"Okay Argo, I'm glad you are listening. I will be more specific - and use my own life at the point of my relapse into alcoholism to provide an example that illustrates this. I was a monsignor of a parish and believed passionately that I should devote myself completely to the care of the church and parishioners of which I had charge. While doing pastoral counseling, I had become very close to a beautiful young woman from the parish and against all my training and moral beliefs, I became her lover. In addition, to assuage my anxiety about all the trauma and sadness that had occurred in my life, I had started using alcohol again and was drinking myself into oblivion every night. Yours truly, the Fr. John who now stands before you, was essentially three different people: a priest who functioned logically, an alcoholic trying to drown his emotional suffering, and a man satisfying his physical needs via an illicit sexual relationship. I completely failed in my duties and responsibilities as a priest, as a partner to the woman I supposedly loved, and to myself. Can you see why?"

"Actually John, I can sort of understand it, but I cannot explain it. Can you?"

"Yes, but you will have to listen with a 'new' set of ears to apprehend the explanation. It exists outside the realm of current theoretical views of human behavior, yet it provides an explanation for the insanity that surrounds us on all sides. Are you ready?"

Argo gestured for the priest to continue.

"Human beings are not taught that they possess three thought centers, but each of us does. We have a physical center that regulates our body and all its needs and functions, then we have an emotional center that includes our feelings and desire to love and be loved, and finally we have our thinking center. Most of us concentrate on one of our centers, and pretty much act as if the other two don't exist - that is where the trouble begins. You may wish to live a thoughtful life, but if you are ignoring your physical needs, they will surprise you when they spring up and occasionally take control. The same with emotions - you may wish operate logically, and never take your feelings into account, but then all of a sudden they take over."

Argo responded.

"So your crash and burn at the church wasn't the drinking?"

"No Argo - it was the scattered ''being" I brought to my life. I was certain that I could think and reason my way through life's issues, and gave no attention to my emotional or physical parts of myself. Those parts of me were vitally alive - they didn't just shut down because I ignored them. While I was logically running the parish, my physical self was longing for expression with a lover, and my tortured emotional self was seeking relief in alcohol. I could never be in control, because I was living as if my logical brain was in charge. I was completely beaten and had to confront that I was both powerless and likely to repeat the same insane mistakes again. I saw no way out, because I didn't understand the complex forces that operated within or how to master them."

Argo was fascinated.

"Obviously you found your way out - how?"

"It might be more accurate to say I was given the keys to solve the problem - the only credit I can take is that I was ready to receive them and I have worked and continue to work very, very hard to acquire a certain mastery. If you have an interest, I'll tell you about it."

Argo's was fascinated by what the priest was relating.

"I would very much like to hear about it."

Fr. John seemed pleased.

"Okay - I'll give you the high points. It unfolded in a very serendipitous way. The Church had relieved me of my duties in the parish and sent me to a facility they maintain for clergy in crisis - a monastery in the rural South. One day

I happened to sit next to a very old monk at the morning meal. He was recuperating at the monastery from an illness he had developed during his travels in the U. S. He was from Tibet. He was not of the Catholic faith, but had come from a monastic order in Tibet where a very ancient spiritual practice had been carried on for millenniums. Although he was very old, he possessed a loving and wise presence that seemed to radiate from the center of his being and touched everyone around him. I was surprised when the old monk invited me to take a walk with him in the forest after our meal. For no reason I could articulate, it seemed somehow important that I do so. He led the way, taking us along a trail several miles into the woods that surrounded the monastery. Eventually we came to a clearing with two stones in the center - he motioned for me to sit on one, then he took a place on the other. For a few moments he simply looked at me. It was a very strange experience - he seemed able to see inside me, but in a very gentle and loving way. Suddenly and without preface he addressed me using my military rank and surname from my days as a special operations soldier.

> 'Ensign Sterling, you have strived your whole life to live honorably and to care for those around you. Yet your efforts have always failed. Your military service put you in the middle of slaughter and chaos. You tried to escape that, but became an alcoholic and drug addict. You refused to give up and focused on freeing yourself from that slavery. You made a promise to God that you would devote your life to saving the spiritual lives of others, and dedicated all

> of your strength to become a priest. But you have failed again, and now see that you must always fail. You realize that you are the cause of your own failure, and that if you continue as you have in the past, it can only lead to more failure. If you wish to escape the endless cycle to which you are now doomed, you must adopt wisdom you do not now possess. If you are willing, I will teach you.'

I was stunned by his words and how he clearly saw everything about my life. I blurted out:

> 'How could you know all these things about me?'

The old monk's kindly expression was replaced by a look of disgust - he lashed me with his words – I will always remember them:

> 'You are destined to fail always because your mind is too weak to discern wisdom. I have told you the story of your whole life and offered to guide you past your failures; yet your only response is to question how I could know these things. Rather than accepting that you are confronted with wisdom beyond your understanding that can be a guide for you, you try to reduce it to the useless knowledge you already possess. You are like a blind man stumbling through a mine field. You and the rest of humanity live in virtual darkness with no possibility of escape. Your own impregnable ignorance dooms you.'

His words cut through my mind in one second. It became completely clear that the trap holding me was in my own head. I fell at his feet and begged him to forgive me and become my teacher. Although he had some misgivings about my readiness, he allowed me to become his student. If you look at your experience of me, I suspect you will have no trouble seeing the unity of being the old monk imparted to me. It is probably what convinced you that I could help you in this matter. I cannot briefly summarize what he taught me, but if you are willing, I will impart what I can to you as we work together."

The priest was speaking of something outside the domains of knowledge familiar to Argo.

"So John, I'm getting the idea that this 'unity' of purpose you speak of is not some new slant on commitment or will power. Can you give me even a hint of the essence of it?"

The priest took a moment to compose a reply.

"The path to unity for everyone who embarks upon it, begins with the realization that they have no unity, but behave in response to the random events around us. If we feel ill, or we get a raise at work, or don't get one, if the weather is pleasant, if the stock market is going up, if our favorite sports team wins or loses - it goes on and on. It requires enough introspection and honesty to see that one has spent most of their life mechanically responding to whatever has been placed in their path. That is not what was meant to be. Each of us possesses, deep within ourselves the seed of something, usually long forgotten, that can begin to free us from this. We will call it 'conscience' although it doesn't correspond exactly to the current understanding of that word. The access to this 'conscience' is via a process we will call 'self-remembering'. When a person becomes adept at self-remembering, they tend to live in harmony with themselves and those around them. Random behavior gives way to intentional being. Developing oneself in this manner is a lengthy and difficult process and must be guided by one who has already achieved spiritual unity."

"You can't get there by yourself?" Argo queried.

The looked directly at Argo, and paused deliberately to add emphasis.

"No Argo, you cannot. If you find that you are ready to seek the unity of being of which I speak, you must have a guide. "

Argo was fascinated by what the priest said. He had witnessed the remarkable transformation of this man, and unabashedly admired the resolute power and commitment that radiated from him. Yet, Argo was uncomfortable with the idea of becoming anyone's disciple.

"John... I trust you enough to walk through hell with you, but that doesn't mean I'll put my brain to sleep. I'll agree to operate as if you are my 'flight instructor' in this endeavor, and that everything you say needs to be attended to. I will not promise strict obedience."

The priest weighed how to proceed.

"You are a stubborn mule, but, then, so was I. If you will agree to discuss the issues of this case with me, and be open to my input, then I may be able to get you through this in one piece."

Argo felt relieved.

"Where shall we start?"

Fr. John responded immediately.

"For the present, we will concentrate on clearing up any issues that can become stumbling blocks. The incident last night with Catherine is a good place to start. If you map that experience back to the one I just related to you, it is plain that you have conflicting agendas in play with her. In your work with Praggles, you will constantly be called upon to make critical choices; there will be no margin for error. You must conduct yourself with sure footedness. You must prevent a lapse in purpose that will put you at risk."

Argo understood.

"You think I should discontinue working with Catherine?"

The priest did not hesitate.

"I'll answer your question with two questions. Do you think you can assist her in resolving her romantic transference to you, and do you truly want her to resolve it?"

Argo sat silently for a few moments. He knew he didn't want Catherine to stop being in love with him, and he wracked his mind for a loop-hole that would allow him to justify that. There was none.

"John, you are right. I have become romantically attached to Catherine. It isn't in her best interest for me to continue to treat her when I'm ambivalent about helping her move forward by working through her transference to me. "

The priest said nothing, but continued to gaze at Argo, whose face slowly morphed to an expression of misery.

"Hell John, what I just said is white washed crap. I have fallen in love with her and it is simply and utterly wrong. She is dating someone her own age and I have been critical of him in our sessions. Was I surprised by what happened last night? I pretty much set the whole thing up. "

The priest held up his hand to interrupt Argo.

"Can you see the complete detachment of your thinking self from your emotional and physical self? You must allow me to be a focusing force for you until you are able to do that for yourself. It isn't that you have fallen in love with her, but what you are going to do about it that concerns me. Our spiritual clarity and integrity are our only advantage."

Argo looked puzzled.

"What do you mean John?"

"Simply this - you and I are no match for the power and intellect of Satan. I have studied a number of detailed accounts of exorcisms. The Church maintains detailed records of the interactions between Satan and priests during those rites. The priests who act as exorcists are trained to never act in their own name, but only in the name of God. In every case where a priest has become enraged by Satan's manipulations and attempted to oppose him personally, they were either badly injured or lost their lives."

Argo interrupted.

"They were killed?"

The priest spoke emphatically.

"Yes. You need to know that you are facing that risk."

Argo was struggling to put this together.

"Okay, but this is not the same. This is not an exorcism, Satan or Praggles has come to me with an intention that is not clear. I do not believe he is seeking to pull me into his realm or to prevent anyone from escaping his clutches. Do you see the difference?"

The priest closed his eyes briefly and clasped his hands together. Argo could not tell if he was praying or thinking or both.

"Argo, your observation about his intention may be correct. The nature of his interactions with you are unique, but that does not mean the risks are any less. For instance – think about how exhausting being in Praggles' presence is. Think of a time when you were in the proximity of someone who was in a state of sputtering rage. Remember how some of those feelings seemed to jump over onto you, and how upsetting it was? Being with Satan is similar to that but much riskier. He is like a black hole of self-absorption. His own thought processes are deeply flawed, and he is not restrained by any rules. If he can use you to achieve some dreadful end, he will. Further, if you get careless and he becomes angry with you, he will harm you and perhaps others around you. Do you understand that he can snuff out your life in an instant? You must be completely clear and consistent in your interactions. If you act at cross purposes with him, he will annihilate you."

The priest's words created a clear image for Argo - he shuddered.

"It is dangerous, but I'm not sure I'd disengage even if it was still possible - this is the most astonishing work I've ever had the opportunity to do. Are you suggesting that we try and end this?"

The priest shook his head.

"No, but when one is walking through a minefield, perfect attention is needed to avoid even a single misstep. I agree that this work is groundbreaking; let's give it our undivided attention and work from the strength and grace that flows to us from the Creator. We have to focus ourselves and one another to the task at hand."

"Okay John, I know what I have to do to clean up my side of the street, and will begin by concluding my relationship with Catherine. I will try and salvage some benefit for her from the work she's done with me. I'll let you know how that goes."

"Thanks Argo. It is a rare pleasure to get to work with someone who is as bright, willing and capable as you. Shall we wrap up?"

Argo had something he wished to clear up.

"John, can I ask you a personal question?"

The priest seemed mildly surprised.

"Certainly."

"What is the situation with your daughter and her mother – is seems difficult for you."

The priest hesitated; it was a moment before he spoke.

"My daughter's name is Rachel Lynn; her mother's name is Mary. I love my daughter and have wanted to reach out to her since her birth, but have honored her mother's wish that I do not. I have gotten accustomed to the ache in my heart caused by being separated from the child."

"May I ask what led this arrangement in the first place?"

The priest sighed as he recollected.

"Sure. The triple tiered life I'd been leading was suddenly brought into sharp and public focus, when word leaked out in the parish that Mary was pregnant with my child. I was removed from the position of monsignor at the church, and had to confront the mess I'd created. I never doubted that I wished to remain a priest. It was a terrible time for her and me. Mary interpreted my decision to continue in the priesthood as a personal betrayal; she became quite bitter. When she asked that I not be involved in the child's life, I did not understand what that would mean. Later, when I saw Rachel Lynn in the hospital nursery after her birth a strong, fatherly love sprung up within me."

Argo decided to interject and give the priest a little help.

"John, that sounds very painful. Knowing what you know now, if you had it to do over again, I suspect you would not have agreed to have no contact with your daughter."

"I would have done many things differently, but I try not to think in terms of woulda, shoulda and coulda. It is unproductive."

"So you are whole and complete with Mary and Rachel Lynn?"

"I... no. I continue to try and reach reconciliation with Mary, and I believe one day she will forgive me."

"John, somehow you will find a way to reach her, don't give up."

“Thank you Argo, I won’t.”

The priest looked at his watch, and raised his eyebrows in surprise. Evidently it was later than he thought.

“I am very happy with our meeting today Argo ... I feel we have a chance. I have some parish responsibilities to take care of, so we’ll have to wrap up for now. I will keep you in my prayers and look forward to our next meeting. Let’s touch base by phone every day.”

“Yes.”

They walked to the door of the rectory. As Argo and Fr. John shook hands, the priest put his left arm around Argo’s shoulder and hugged him.

“Bless you.”

And in that moment, Argo felt blessed.

Return to Integrity

The client who usually came before Catherine had cancelled, leaving Argo to fret through the empty hour before her arrival; apprehension permeated his thoughts. She had never been late without calling, and by 8:05pm he began to wonder if she was blowing the session off. The doorman called to announce her arrival a moment later, and Argo sighed with relief.

She rang the office doorbell and he buzzed her into the waiting room, then went to the door of his office to greet her. He wasn't ready for the transformed Catherine who stood before him, and he knew his expression showed it. It was as if each of the natural qualities of loveliness she possessed had been honed, polished and integrated with every other, then accented and enhanced by garments that further coalesced her beauty to hypnotic intensity. She stopped six inches from him - standing tall, shoulders squared, and looked directly into his eyes. The once sweet innocence of her gaze replaced by palpably focused beams that felt like an embrace that sealed them both off from the rest of the world.

After his meetings with Fr. John, Argo had spent many hours thinking through what he wanted to communicate to

Catherine, but had been unable to envision how. Now he knew.

"Well, if I was ever going to make the blunder of falling in love with one of my clients, I'll cling to the excuse that she is the most exquisitely beautiful woman on the planet. You have made some astonishing alterations in your presence - I am glad you are here."

She walked to the sofa, took a seat, then crossed her long legs and patted her skirt down just above the knees. Argo sank into the other end of the couch, half facing her. She continued to look directly into his eyes.

He was conscious of feeling many things - emotional vulnerability, strong physical desire, and a racing stream of impressions. Behind them he was aware of something else - a quiet and warm love for this young woman. He chose this as the source of actions he would take.

She did not wait for him to begin.

"Dr. Masters ... Argo. I am going to call you 'Argo'. Something happened to us in our last session - not just to me, but to both of us. It startled me, and you too. You took me in your arms and there was love in your eyes. You struggled with it, then ended our session saying that we hadn't let it get out of hand and could continue. Do you remember that?"

Argo could feel himself blushing. His client had come a long way - she wasn't relying on his queues any longer.

"Yes Catherine - vividly."

She leaned forward.

"Argo - how exactly do you think we can continue after that? You feel the same way toward me that I feel toward you. You are the only man who ever has taken the time to get to know me. You've shown me a caring and affection that has enabled me to see my place in this world in a whole new way - as a mature woman. From the start I found you attractive. It just grew within me, and now I am in love with you. I sensed it was mutual. Somehow I knew you felt the same way. What are we going to do about it?"

Argo's admiration for her grew even stronger - she spoke exactly what was on her mind, and didn't muddy it up with guilt, apologies, accusations or melodrama.

"Catherine - thank you for your extraordinary candor. I will tell you exactly how I feel and then we can discuss what's best. First of all, I'd like to put what happened last week between us in focus. You said that you were aware of having feelings for me almost since the beginning of our work. I knew I had feelings for you, but mistook them. I knew I wasn't immune to your womanly attractiveness, but judged my feelings for you as being primarily... well... rather fatherly - I was fooling myself. I came to look forward to our sessions with great pleasure, but it never dawned on me how strong my feelings were, until you saw the desire in my eyes, and called me on it. Instantly it all crystalized. It took me a moment to catch myself, and when I did, all I could think to do was try to put the genie back in the bottle. My saying our therapeutic relationship was intact was a reflection of the shock I felt at my own actions. Clearly I had stepped outside the boundaries of the therapeutic relationship in an irreversible manner…".

Catherine had listened intently, but clearly wanted Argo to get past the recap.

"I understand all that, but what now?"

Argo had developed a strong respect for Catherine's ability to handle whatever was placed in her path during their sessions, and he wasn't about to start watering it down now because he was uncomfortable.

"I think it is going to take both of us to figure out where to go from here. When I looked honestly at my feelings, it is clear that I am romantically in love with you. Obviously I cannot treat you. I have wracked my brain with this since our last meeting - I cannot switch from being your therapist, to being your lover."

Catherine's eyes seemed to blaze.

"That is not true! Passionate people sometimes have to cut their own path even if it is outside the normal bounds. I am so surprised that you would let that stop you from being with me!"

Her vehemence rocked him. He had to steady himself and get Catherine to look at this more objectively.

"Whoa counselor - step back a little. You as patient have acted in good faith and are truly blameless. Have you looked at this from my side - as therapist? First - I failed to identify that my countertransference to you had morphed into love. Second, I saw you developing a very strong transference to me, which by the way is quite usual in a therapeutic setting, yet I did nothing to help you resolve it. Would you be in love with me if I had not been your therapist? Thirdly, I have been in a committed relationship for twelve years. She and I aren't married, but we've been exclusive by choice.

For the first time, Catherine seemed flustered.

"I hadn't considered that there might be someone else. When I asked you about your life, you never mentioned that."

"A therapist's self-disclosure has to be minimal; the focus is on you - the client."

"You are young and vibrant with a beauty and intelligence that is magnified a thousand times by your huge heart. Your lovingness permeates everything you do, it is who you are. My deep feelings for you began when I recognized that quality in you. I have utilized my skills, maturity, understanding and love in our work to help you make the transitions you sought, not to seduce you.

Aside from your career, you are the possibility of children and family, but not with me. I am twenty five years your senior - old enough to be your father, and will be an old man while you are still young. I would feel like Dracula using up your youthfulness to energize my life."

Tears welled in her eyes, and spilled down her cheeks.

"I don't care about your age – I want to be with you, and you know you want to be with me!"

Argo wondered how his life could have become so convoluted that he was pushing this amazing woman away from him. He could neither end the relationship nor see a way to engage in it. He stared at the floor and searched for something to say. Unaccountably a thought about Praggles and the work he and Fr. John were doing crossed his mind – it helped him regain some sense of perspective.

Catherine had gotten the gist of Argo's struggle as much from his tone of voice and demeanor as his words. She had looked away and stared out the window and continued to do so for a moment – utter silence filled the office. Finally she spoke.

"You and I never talked like this in our sessions, but I find myself not being surprised. I could have guessed you would choose as you have. I get it, but I feel sad, and I feel alone. In the last five or six months, you were always there for me to vent, or look for answers, or simply to talk. What happens now – do I walk out of your office and we never see or speak to one another again?"

Argo knew that severing all communication with Catherine would be the text book answer, but that felt completely wrong. Not having a precedent for how to handle this, he did what he usually did - went with his gut.

"No, not unless you would prefer that. I believe the best outcome for us would be to find a way to resolve this conundrum and honor our caring for each other. There is something in my connection with you that has nourished me to the bottom of my soul. I'm feeling my way along on this, but your caring, the vibration of your womanliness and the warmth you generously give me changes everything. I sense that you have felt something similar from me. I propose that we give ourselves the benefit of the doubt and try something unorthodox. May I tell you what I'm thinking?"

Catherine seemed fascinated.

"Okay..."

Argo began.

"Step one is a reality check. We take a forty day sabbatical to gain perspective and collect our thoughts. During this time we refrain from being in contact. If your love for me is authentic, and mine for you - the sabbatical will not blunt it. If it isn't, then so be it. After the sabbatical, we meet and tell each other what we've discovered. If the bond between us endures, then we can choose how we will be in one another's life."

Catherine seemed puzzled by something.

"Why forty days?"

Argo knew she would ask.

"It matches the forty days Christ fasted in the desert before being tempted by Satan – it seemed appropriate."

She laughed.

"I am often surprised by the way your mind works, but I believe this is a good way to proceed."

She stood up to leave, and Argo rose with her. She stepped towards him, took his face in both her hands, kissed him softly on the mouth, then walked to the door.

"Argo - I'll see you in forty days."

As she exited, he repeated a phrase to himself that often cheered him up:

"Hear ye, hear ye - life is in session!"

Randall

HE WAITED WHILE RANDALL seated himself. His client unholstered his iPhone and handed it to Argo, who smiled in acknowledgment, and placed it in the top center drawer of his desk. He remembered how his client had referenced the device continuously during their first sessions, until Argo had demanded he surrender it at the beginning of every meeting. He wondered if the day would come when he would have to remind Randall to take it back at the end of a visit. He could hear a staccato beat and muffled rap lyrics coming from the ear buds of his client's iPod, as he popped them out of his ears and turned it off. Randall began drumming on the forward edge of his seat with his forefingers and looked at Argo expectantly. At first Argo had experienced difficulty in working with Randall, but had reminded himself of a primary tenet of his profession – if you show people a better way to live, they will take it. Within a few visits he had developed such an empathy with Randall that he looked forward to their sessions. It was mutual.

Argo glanced at the notes he'd made at the end of their last session:

Reinforce good thinking with good actions
Strengthen vision for the future

Work to reduce risk

Randall was 24, gay and had moved to New York several years ago after completing college. He was from a small town on the coast of Maine where, as far as he knew, nobody else was gay. He had never acknowledged his sexual orientation even to himself until a year ago. He had repressed his sexuality out of terror; having been taught that homosexuals were deviant and detestable. That ended one night when he had gotten drunk and wandered into a gay bar. In a matter of weeks he had fallen in with a rough young gay crowd, had begun using methamphetamine, and having frequent, compulsive sexual encounters. He was referred to Argo by a mutual acquaintance after taking an overdose of sedatives in a failed suicide attempt. Randall's new life style had filled him with self-loathing. Argo had ruled out psychosis and personality disorders early on. An analysis of Randall's drug use convinced Argo that his client had not yet developed a dependency, but would if he continued to use them. He developed a treatment plan focused on minimizing the dangers inherent in his current life style, ending his use of non-prescription drugs, reducing the compulsive sexual encounters, stabilizing Randall by defusing the self-loathing, then helping him on his path of self-acceptance and discovery. Randall had shown an openness and willingness to engage in the inquiry of leading a great life that Argo had introduced, and was making good progress.

Argo looked up, focused his gaze on Randall's eyes, slowly allowed a warm and conspiratorial smile to spread across his face, and began.

"So Randall, I've been wondering all week if you were going to make your move with the roller disco. Tell me how that's going."

Randall's features became happily animated, he raised his arms in a gesture of victory and half shouted.

"I did it, I did it! They loved me, oh my God was I scared, but once I started there was no stopping me. I just danced like a maniac. And I didn't use meth to get me out there either."

Randall had been drawn to the roller disco party in Central Park that went on all weekend, every weekend in a paved area just south of the Bethesda Fountain. He loved to dance, and was a good skater, but lacked the confidence to go out with the other skaters. Argo wanted to aid Randall in the area of self-expression as a way of boosting his self-esteem, and the roller disco seemed a good opportunity. The biggest block to spontaneous self-expression is performance anxiety born of self-consciousness. Argo had coached Randall using techniques borrowed from acting classes to help him overcome his fear. It was based on the premise that in all authentic communication, one must be willing to appear anywhere on the spectrum from idiot to genius. It is natural to want to look good, but the self-monitoring that engenders sucks all the spontaneity out of what we say and do. The technique to overcome this was simple – it involved reciting and acting out a ridiculous dialogue designed to make one appear foolish. In this manner one could get over the need to 'look good' and begin to communicate and behave naturally. Argo had dredged up a routine specifically designed for men that involved acting like 'Betty Boop' while reciting the following lines:

Tight little curls
Turned up nose
Hot curvy figure
Form fitting clothes.
Tiny waist
Cute little bum
Lookout boys
Here I come!

Randall had resisted the idea until Argo modeled the routine for him. It had taken Argo three tries to get it perfectly, but that had helped his client see the process. Randall had roared with laughter when Argo nailed the Betty Boop routine. He dug into it with enthusiasm and with a little coaching was doing a hilariously vibrant Betty.

Argo felt both pleased and relieved that Randall had been able to bring the freedom of expression he'd mastered in their session to the roller disco in the park; he sometimes angsted about client's problems more than they did. He nodded his head empathically.

"Good for you Randall, good for you. I know what it took for you to get out there, and am proud of you. Did Dr. Horrible give you much trouble?"

Dr. Horrible was the name Randall had given to his self-loathing. Part of Argo's approach had been to encourage him to see the loathing as external to himself, and naming it was part of the process. It enabled Randall put a little distance between him and the problem in a helpful way.

Randall laughed and replied.

"Dr. Horrible started off by suggesting I snort a little meth to help get my motor going. I decided not to, but when I got there he shot his whole load! There were some awesome dancers out there and he was saying things like: 'Who's gonna look at your scrawny faggot ass when they can watch those guys?' and 'Just what the roller disco needs – a clown.' I remembered what you said about being willing to be myself, whether that turned out to be a fool or a genius. I let the music in, I let it take over, and when it did – I skated out and just danced and danced. Dr. Horrible vanished!"

Argo knew this was a major opportunity to do some exploring that would allow Randall to see strengths and character traits that were not normally visible to him. He gazed quietly at Randall for a moment and let the silence add a reflective aura to the space between them.

"I am inspired by the way you are standing for yourself. I wonder if this reminds you of anything. Can you think of other times when you overcame feelings of fear and self-loathing?"

Randall's brow knit as he thought, then he tilted his head to one side and began speaking; slowly at first, then more rapidly.

"You know...it does. It's not quite the same, but somehow it reminds me of this. It happened when I was thirteen. My dad had made my little brother and me go to sailing camp. After six weeks, all the kids who started sailing that summer were ranked as 'First Mates.' That meant we could do anything on the boat, except be the skipper. We could raise and lower the sails, steer it, trim the sails, and pick up a mooring - all that stuff. Well, about that time some of the older kids who were the skippers and who taught us, had to go off to college. Now there weren't enough skippers for the boats and there were three weeks of sailing left. The head of the program had a meeting with all the first mates and asked if any of us thought we were ready to be skippers. We were all so surprised by the question that nobody said anything. Then he drew an imaginary line on the floor and said 'Anybody who thinks they are ready right now to be a skipper – step across the line.' I wanted to be a skipper in the worst way, but was scared I might not know enough, or that the other kids would laugh at me. I stepped across the line anyway; I was the only one who did."

Argo asked.

"And what happened?"

Randall's face reflected the power the recollection still had for him.

"He appointed me a skipper and gave me a crew of two new kids. I spent the rest of the summer teaching them to sail."

Argo loved this part of his work; he wasn't pumping his client up with empty praise; but reconnecting him with lost memories that would allow him to see his own courage and worth. He continued with the inquiry.

"Wow! That is an amazing story. You made a choice to seize what you wanted, risked ridicule and failure, and pulled it off. Can you think of another time when you have made an out of the box choice?"

Randall didn't hesitate this time.

"Your question has gotten me thinking about a bunch of choices like that. The college I attended was not the one the guidance counselor at my school or my parents picked. My choice to take a job in New York City was like that too. Funny how I forgot about all of those things."

Argo knew that it was far from 'funny'. His life and work had illustrated time and again how human beings live within the context of the narrative they have constructed of their lives, and if that story is a dead end, then every event they experience is filtered through 'dead end'. Virtually no light can get in, and dead end becomes a self-fulfilling prophecy. What he was now doing with Randall was a process called 'thickening' in which the therapist helps the client find and utilize recollections from their lives that present a picture outside the dead-end story. The client can then construct a narrative whose context allows for satisfaction and fulfillment. Argo continued.

"So what do these choices say about you as a person?"

Randall became thoughtful for a moment before replying.

"Well, for one, I don't follow the pack. I didn't see that before, but you know what? It's accurate!"

Argo concurred.

"Randall, it is clear that you do not follow the crowd in your thinking and are willing to step outside the box when necessary. What quality do you think it takes to step outside of the box?"

Randall didn't reply immediately. Argo could see he had connected with something.

"It takes courage."

Argo clapped his hands in a heartfelt applause.

"Bingo"! Randall blushed slightly and they both laughed.

In the beginning of their session Randall had mentioned his decision not to use crystal meth in his roller disco debut, and Argo used it now to segue to an intervention in that domain. Argo considered the 12-step-recovery programs of Alcoholics Anonymous and Narcotics Anonymous to be the gold standard of treatment for both substance abuse and dependence. They didn't work for everybody, but worked amazingly well for those who could embrace their structure. Argo kept a pack of Narcotics Anonymous and Alcoholics Anonymous meeting lists in the file drawer of his desk, and he selected one and put it on his desk.

"Randall, I'd like you to accompany me to a Narcotics Anonymous Meeting if we can find one that fits both our schedules. It would give you a leg up on handling the crystal meth. Would you be willing to do that?"

By the end of their session, Randal and Argo had found a meeting that suited them both. Argo felt that bringing clients to a first meeting was the best way to insure both attendance and a good first impression. At the conclusion of their session, he walked Randall out to the waiting room.

The Rant

PRAGGLES SAT ON THE COUCH in the waiting room, and came to his feet as Randall passed by him and exited to the outside hallway. He turned to Argo and began.

"That is the walking embodiment of the pitiful state of humanity. He is 24 years old yet retains a state of consciousness and awareness of a child. He has no interest in anything beyond satisfying his desire for sex, attention and mindless titillation. He is the future."

Argo smiled at the irony of having Randall critiqued by a fellow client. Praggles seeming knowledge of Argo and his other patients had been disconcerting at first, but also provided insights into his mysterious client.

Praggles did not sit down immediately, but paced in front of Argo; he continued to speak about Randall.

"Are you aware that his cell phone is connected to a service that electronically assists him in finding, and selecting partners like himself for random sexual encounters? It employs GPS technology to provide their locations, and gives him profiles of relevant physical characteristics and preferences upon request. He has three or four hookups on some days - people he does not know and will never see again."

Two things occurred to Argo as his client spoke; he detected something underneath the anger in Praggles speaking, and it was also clear that he had not accessed Argo's feelings for or knowledge of Randall. Argo watched his own emotions and feelings at the same time and detected a gut level tension, which had not yet become distinct enough for words. He chose to proceed solely on the basis of expanding his client's insight.

"It appears that Randall has been kind enough to accelerate our session. I felt your anger. Can you speak about that?"

Praggles became very still. Argo felt a spike of emotional energy emanate from his client, but the only alteration in his demeanor was a sharpening of the focus of his eyes.

"Anger? I would have said contempt, but yes, you are accurate. He gets up in the morning and takes anti-anxiety medication to dull his feelings. He puts his headphones on and plays music videos, while he scans his text messages and activates his profiles to notify everyone in his 'networks' that he is online. If he goes to his job, every instant he is not doing the mindless busy work he is tasked with, he continues with this routine, or augments it with the automated sexual networking. If you are thinking that this is just a stage that young people pass through, you are not watching what is right under your nose."

Argo didn't miss the irony in his client's admonition, however he did not agree with Praggles assessment of the irretrievable hopelessness of Randall's existence. He sensed that Praggles either could not access how he felt about Randall, or simply had no interest.

Praggles wasn't finished.

"Large numbers of your fellow adults are doing the same thing. They clutter their consciousness digesting useless bombardments of information from news and sports media, engaging in fantasy football, being sucked into meaningless controversies, scanning the web for pornography, filling out questionnaires for dating services to find possible new partners, shopping for the day's bargains, and engaging in an infinite number of other available activities to distract themselves from ever having to deal with anything of real substance. They think they are alive, but they have not yet arrived on the playing field of life, and seem determined to avoid ever making an appearance there."

Argo nodded and affirmed Praggles' observations.

"When you state it that way it brings home the pervasiveness of the phenomenon. To occupy ones consciousness solely with activities and ruminations of the unendingly trivial seems such a waste."

Praggles response let Argo know that his affirmation had not been sufficient.

"A waste...it is far more than a waste..."

Argo had sensed that Praggles complaints were the tip of the iceberg; that he was as yet unwilling or unable to articulate what his real issues were. It was time to move the process along.

"Can you tell me why you say that?"

The question caused a particularly acute emotional spike from Praggles. He seemed ambivalent for a moment, but then began to speak.

"I will illustrate what I mean by telling you of an event that occurred three years ago at a campsite between two mountain villages in Afghanistan. It was early evening; five brothers who had been traveling together on their return to their village from a friend's wedding in a nearby city. They were cooking a meal before sleeping. Unbeknownst to them, an unmanned drone several thousand feet above was observing them. The drone transmitted visual data as well as sensor readings to a satellite link that passed them on to a combat command center at an military base in Utah. The technician controlling the drone maneuvered it to get a closer look. The men carried rifles, as do most men in that region. The technician noted that they were armed and camping on a mountain trail, thereby meeting two criteria on a checklist of characteristics for identifying enemy combatants. The drone's sensors then indicated the presence of sophisticated communications equipment associated with surface to air missiles. This item completed the checklist's criteria for positive identification of enemy combatants. The technician communicated the sensor readings to his superiors and received clearance to 'neutralize' the personnel in the camp. He initiated the drone's automated targeting processes, and then activated the attack sequence when notified that the target had been locked in. Several seconds later a missile from the drone exploded in the midst of the camp; all five brothers were killed instantly."

Argo winced at the story; flashing back to hearing the first plane exploding into the North Tower of the World Trade Center. He knew this was different, but did not have enough information to reach any conclusions.

"Warfare and sudden death. Five lives ended; it seems so senseless. Yet this is the nature of war, I suspect there is another piece in the puzzle."

Praggles replied.

"What you are missing, is the one piece of information necessary to appreciate what actually happened. The drone's sensor readings for the presence of advanced communications hardware was manufactured by the software, they were not real. The software was programmed by someone you would describe as a geek, who chose to insert random false positives into the combat drone surveillance software for his own amusement. He is a very highly intelligent and well-educated software engineer, who, like many of his associates, has no grounding in morality, and no awareness of anything beyond what his logical mind can apprehend. The men who died on the trail are no more significant to him than the characters in a video game. He belongs to a loose association of hackers who have risen to influential positions in various firms and government agencies across the globe. They compete with each other to see who can cause the most spectacular aberrations without getting caught."

The story was appalling to Argo, but still made no sense in the context of explaining Praggles fear. Argo pressed.

"I still don't get what concerns you about that. They were murdered by evil perpetrated by another human being. Why would that be an issue for you?"

Praggles answered without hesitation.

"The commission of evil requires knowledge of right and wrong. The perpetrator lacks that knowledge. He is not even in the game. Does that begin to give you an idea of what the problem is here?"

Praggles became quiet, but Argo could feel an almost unbearable stream of emotional energy building like an unuttered scream within him. He decided to bring his client into contact with his feelings.

"I would like to change the focus of our conversation back to you. Specifically, the effect this act had on you. Are you willing to explore that?"

Praggles nodded in the affirmative but gazed at him warily. Argo proceeded.

"You noted at our first meeting that our conversations would have the effect of depleting my energy. You have ended our two previous sessions when you sensed I lacked the energy to continue. Do you remember?"

Praggles shrugged.

"Yes, why do you ask?"

Argo responded.

"I will explain. Obviously, as a spiritual being you are unique among my clients. Based on our conversations, I had presumed that you would not experience volatility in your moods and feelings; however I have been surprised to observe that you exhibit strong emotional responses. I believe that my weariness during our sessions resulted from the energy required to deal with your emotional projections. Does this agree with your experience of our conversations?"

Praggles regarded Argo curiously for several seconds, then, as if remembering the framework in which they were communicating, a puzzled look passed over his features, but was quickly replaced with a cold, emotionless mask. His voice was controlled and deliberately paced when he replied.

"Emotions and feelings are not significant in the spiritual domain. We may experience them, but they would have negligible influence. I am surprised you mention it."

He wondered if Praggles was warning him not to 'go there'. He decided to proceed.

"I brought it up because it may be important. I can feel your presence when you enter the room, and it is at that point my energy begins to drain. When we converse, it is clear when you are experiencing emotions - I feel it intensely. At the beginning of our session, as you spoke about Randall, you released a large quantity of emotional energy. This projection of emotion increased when you told me of the five brothers being murdered in the mountains. What were you feeling when you spoke?"

Praggles' face became completely expressionless, almost like a wax mask. Argo had seen this several times before and sensed he had become so engrossed in processing the question that he was not attending to his physical manifestation. After a moment a watchful expression appeared on Praggles' face and he queried Argo.

"You say you feel intense emotional projection from me at times when we speak. I am unaware of any emotional content in my communication. What emotions do you feel I project?"

Argo suddenly felt like a soldier who discovers he is in the center of a minefield. He was always reluctant to provide clients with his opinion about their experience, but had no doubt that Praggles was unaware of his emotions. That was often true with anger issues. The subject would feel so justified in their anger that it seemed an appropriate and logical response, rather than an emotionally based one. Clearly Praggles shared this delusion. Although Argo was reluctant to communicate his thoughts he found himself doing so without any attempt to soften the impact.

"Anger is definitely projected, and underneath the anger is a second emotion. Would it surprise you if I said 'fear'?"

Suddenly Argo felt himself being crushed. His ribs were cracking and he could not breathe. He saw Praggles' face contort hideously, as he hissed.

"I am afraid? You insignificant worm!"

Whatever he said next was not recognizable. Argo fell forward face down on his desk and lost consciousness. He did not know how long he had been out when he returned to a semi-conscious state; his ears were filled with the sound of his own panting breath. He did not have the energy to raise his head from the desk for several moments, and felt blood ooze from his nose and puddle by his cheek.

When Argo sat up, Praggles was on his feet, peering at him. He seemed to be trying to decide what to say. Argo held up his hand to indicate he should not speak. He cleared his throat.

"One of the things you agreed to as a condition of our working together was that neither I, nor anyone associated with me would be harmed as a result. That is our contract, and you have broken it. What you did has hurt me. Do you understand that?"

Praggles seemed to marvel at Argo's words, but just nodded his head slowly. After a moment a chilling smile appeared on his face and he began to laugh.

"I am getting quite an education today Dr. Masters. First you tell me that I am prone to anger and fear, then admonish me for not following the terms of what you so charmingly call our contract. I must say you have always fascinated me, when you decide to do something; you don't look to the left or to the right, but just proceed. You, a mere man, are actually seriously attempting to provide me with psychotherapy."

Praggles laughed, but only for a few seconds, then his expression transitioned to brooding and reflective. He continued.

"A moment ago I almost killed you; that action, as you have so accurately pointed out, was driven by anger. I cannot convey how surprised I am to learn that anger can cause me to act thoughtlessly."

Argo interjected.

"Congratulations! You have experienced your first therapeutic insight."

Argo wiped the blood from his cheek with a napkin he had dampened from a bottle of drinking water as he continued.

"You are correct that I have acted as your therapist, and have done so without reservation. The contract we made allowed me to do that. What made it possible for me to focus on your concerns without distraction are the agreements we made. Therapy often has the effect of arousing strong emotions, and evidently that is true for spiritual beings also. Having said that - it is not my intention to die while working with you."

Argo could feel another surge of energy coming from Praggles, but it ceased almost before it began.

He spoke musingly.

"Our conversations have been the most difficult I have ever had. Answering your questions has required that I assume the posture of an equal; it is not what I was created to do. That I sought you out in the first place is outside the limits of the behaviors proscribed for me, but I have caused it to occur. Your assertions about anger and fear; for an instant I lost control. You tell me this is a normal part of this process, but you will not survive another such interaction. We had best conclude our business Dr. Masters."

Argo experienced mixed feeling at Praggles' decision; relief and regret, but the regret was stronger. Argo was a born therapist; once he connected with a client, his mind never stopped wondering, theorizing, drafting interventions and focusing on the life, circumstances and possibilities for that individual. He had definitely connected with Praggles. He collected his thoughts as he looked into Praggles eyes. He cleared his throat, and then spoke.

"May I ask why you didn't kill me?"

Praggles shook his head wearily.

"You should be able to deduce that from our discussions don't you think?"

Argo felt his own anger rising, perhaps born of frustration - his track record for deducing Praggles motives was poor.

"You didn't kill me because that is not your function. Is that the only reason?"

Praggles said nothing for a moment.

"It is a reason, and the only one I will provide."

Either Praggles did not want him to know, or wanted him to figure it out for himself. He decided to let it go, and to say what was there for him. He hoped it would provide his client with what he needed.

"I admire the courage you showed to begin this, and will tell you frankly that I experience being privileged to have taken part in your exploration. In my business, we have learned that both the therapist and the patient are changed in the process. You have given me a perspective on spiritual matters beyond anything I could have ever hoped to attain. It is a precious gift, and you have my gratitude for it. Our conversations have also brought you insights into your own motives that were not available to you before. We have come this far, but clearly have only scratched the surface of what is possible. What would it mean if you could speak of the things that concern you? I leave the door open for us to continue if you can do so without taking my life."

Argo felt a strange energy flowing from Praggles who had risen to his feet and was gathering up his coat.

"This will be our last conversation; it is time for me to leave. Good bye Dr. Masters."

Praggles did not go through the charade of exiting through the door - he simply vanished. The room was as quiet as if it had been deserted for some time.

Argo had no way of knowing if Praggles would return; there was a lot of unfinished business between them. He hoped he would. Argo was much too tired to leave the office. He had agreed to call Fr. John when the session was over; the priest answered his cell on the first ring. Argo briefly described the session. His friend was extremely concerned, but reluctantly agreed to wait to meet till breakfast the next morning. Argo pulled the blanket out of his lower drawer, kicked off his shoes, shut out the light, and lay down on the couch. He was asleep instantly.

Aftermath

ARGO WAS STIFF AND SORE the next morning, but aside from being somewhat weary, felt whole. His wrinkled clothing, unshaven face and un-showered body reminded him of his drinking days, when he would stay out all night then go to work. Fr. John had looked him over carefully when they met, and then listened in fascination as he related the details of the session with Praggles. As usual, he jotted notes on a small pad. When Argo finished, he stared at him pensively for a moment.

"You took a huge risk. It's a miracle that you still breathing! What were you thinking?

"I'm not sure where to begin. It is my impression that Praggles is tortured by some vision, and that is his primary reason for coming to me. I think he lives in dread, although I cannot say why - it is a gut feeling I've had almost from the beginning. As far as his contempt for humanity, it may be just so, but I also sense jealousy.

His psychological makeup is where I struggle the most. While I cannot attempt to evaluate him by human standards, he seems to share a number of distinctly human characteristics. For instance, his subjective point of view; he has the same blind spots with regard to his own motives as most of us. His visceral dislike of Randall didn't make sense; Randall was raised with a solid grounding in morality and faith. He knows the difference between right and wrong. I read Praggles contempt for Randall as more mood related than logical. He is very affected by anger and fear yet doesn't see it. I suspect that those two emotional states have been continually present within him for so long that they seem normal to him. He is unable to distinguish them the same way a child can't get the concept of air – it is so everywhere they've never noticed it. What I cannot get at is distinguishing what he really wants. I think he gave me some of the pieces, but it just hasn't jelled.

In terms of his ability to read my mind - he seems to be limited to those thoughts he can understand. He has no ability to sense warmth, affection or concern. He seemed stunned when he discovered that I was actually trying to treat him. He had never considered it - even though I plainly was. That is about all I can say at this point. Tell me what you see."

Fr. John scanned Argo's face, and collected his thoughts. He began almost haltingly.

"We are both feeling our way along here, the scope of the issues surrounding your client is unprecedented. When Praggles expressed surprise that you were genuinely trying to treat him, I felt the same way. I am a priest, and although I'm a pastoral counselor too, I am a priest first. The idea of interacting with him in anything but a defensive posture is very new territory. I agree with your assessment that he is suffering. It is what God intended - it is the consequence of his rebellion. My sense is that he does not like the way things are going with humankind, because he sees something that hurts or threatens him. It is something so dreadful that he cannot face it let alone articulate it. When you intervened to help him become more aware, he nearly choked the life out of you. In spite of his posturing as a benefactor of humanity, I see no evidence to suggest he is operating out of anything but narrow self-interest. Is there some reason you think he won't take your life next time?"

Argo responded to the priest's concern.

"I have a sense this isn't finished. I don't know if Praggles will come back, but if he does, I'll be there. You know that I've led a pretty blessed life. There are so many times I should have died for the foolish way I lived, yet I was always granted the grace to come out the other end of any dilemma I'd enmeshed myself in. You know how far down alcoholism took me, and the serendipitous way recovery came my way. I don't know what is going on, but my sense is that this work has been put in front of us for a reason."

Fr. John responded.

"Have you considered that Praggles' may be using you as a conduit?"

Argo was fascinated by the priest's supposition.

"Say more."

"Okay. In the second session, he stated that he had no direct contact with the Creator. Do you remember?"

Argo nodded.

"Yes."

"Do you remember the story of Job in the Old Testament? Job loved and worshipped the Creator with utter devotion. More than any other human being he enjoyed God's favor, yet he suddenly lost everything. His wealth was taken, all his children died, his friends turned their backs on him, even his wife mocked him, and his health failed. He was completely bewildered and had no idea what was happening. He had no idea he was the unwitting, but central character in a drama playing out between God and Satan."

Argo remembered it now, but wasn't sure why the priest saw a connection.

"What exactly are you saying?"

"Praggles has made the point several times that he has no direct communication with the Creator, but has said that he has observed your connection with the Creator as strong. Do you remember that?"

Argo recalled Praggles alluding to the connection when he asked him whether the creator would be offended if he worked with him. He nodded.

The priest continued.

"He has also alluded to an instance in your life where there was a spiritual intervention that saved you from certain death. I'm speaking of the event that occurred when you were twenty two years old, where a disembodied voice commanded you to stop the car you were driving on a dark, rainy highway. Had you not stopped you would have collided with the enormous boulder that blocked the road. Remember that?"

Argo could see where the priest was headed.

"You're right, and last night when I asked him why he didn't kill me, he refused to elaborate. Although I cannot imagine myself being involved in a Job like conversation between the Creator and Satan, neither have I been able to account for the voice that intervened to save my life that night. Over the years I've been the beneficiary of more than a few miracles. The things I've seen have been so striking that their meaning even penetrated my thick skull. When Praggles left last night he said he would not return. I don't know why, but I'd be surprised if this was the end of our interactions. I pray for wisdom and beg you to pray on my behalf. I know this isn't about me. The most astonishing part of this is that interacting with Praggles has crystalized my faith - and changed it."

"Really?" The priest asked.

"Praggles makes plain the utter poverty of existence without love. But beyond that - in my personal search for God, and studying scripture, I had sensed something missing. Praggles has pointed to that throughout our sessions. Actually, you have also in your speaking about yourself and the old monk. I am beginning to see the outlines of something that fills me with a sense of mystery and anticipation."

Fr. John reached over and put his hand on Argo's forearm.

"I understand your sense that this must be played out. Go home now and rest. The only thing that is clear at the moment is that we must keep putting one foot in front of the other."

Argo and the priest spoke a little longer, and then parted company. Argo had clients scheduled for the afternoon and needed to go home and clean up, before returning to the office. He also wanted to attend an AA meeting; they always helped him regain a sense of being part and parcel with the rest of humanity.

Teasers

ARGO FELT CERTAIN THAT HE AND PRAGGLES would meet again. From a therapeutic standpoint, their work had proceeded well, and Praggles, for all his struggling, had been able to face and acknowledge the fear that afflicted him. He sensed that after untold ages of solitude, there had been catharsis for this dark, cold spirit, and after once beginning, he would not interrupt the process. For Argo, being part of Praggles' cosmic inquiry was the most exciting and challenging work of his life. He half expected Praggles to appear in his waiting room late some night, but as the days stretched into weeks that didn't happen.

Argo and Fr. John continued to meet on Friday mornings. They had lived immersed in a world that took for granted that their most cherished beliefs were antiquated and irrelevant, and over time, little by little, each had been enervated by the exposure. Ironically Praggles had turned that around. The single most intriguing feature of the mystery for both men was that Satan would be haunted by the disappearance of spirituality. Why? They used their time together to probe every nuance of the therapy sessions for clues. What began to emerge was a profile of a spirit that resembled the traditional depictions in some ways, but not others, and whose motives and purpose remained tantalizingly beyond their reach. Praggles was a shadow of the monstrous and wretchedly intrepid rebel of 'Paradise Lost'; there was a big crack in his defiance.

It was prior to one of the breakfast meetings a month after Praggles' final session with Argo that they realized that contact had been renewed. The priest arrived several minutes late; he appeared frazzled and was shaking his head. When Argo observed that the priest seemed upset, Fr. John said a man had just accosted him as he was waiting for the walk signal to cross the street. The man had been waving a newspaper, and insisted that the priest listen to him rant about an article that detailed an apparently accidental shipment of nuclear warheads from an Air Force base in Washington State to another base in Texas. According to the article, the weapons had been shipped without security or precautions of any kind; the weapons were recovered, but nobody seemed to know who had authorized the transfer. When the man finished speaking, he handed the priest the paper with the article circled, then turned abruptly and walked away.

The look on Argo's face stopped Fr. John in mid-sentence.

"What did the man look like?"

"He was dressed in a black suit, overweight, sort of dull looking. He spoke rapidly, like he was excited, but his eyes seemed...well...porcine and at the same time empty...almost dead. Why do you ask?"

The priest expression had morphed from annoyance to puzzlement.

Argo could not conceal his excitement.

"John, that man stopped me in the street two days ago in White Plains and told me the same story. I was up there for a seminar. I think this is what we've been waiting for."

The priest understood immediately.

"The messenger must have been one of the 'minions' Praggles referred to in several of his conversations with you. Unless this is some mad coincidence, Praggles has reestablished communications with you...actually with us!"

Argo nodded.

"Praggles has decided to continue the work he started. I believe he is laying the groundwork for our next meeting."

They spent the next hour going over everything Praggles had said in his sessions with Argo, looking for some connection to the story about the warhead shipment. The thread eluded them.

The next message arrived a week later and was delivered verbally to Fr. John in a fashion that made the identity of the sender unmistakable. The messenger appeared to be a boy in his early teens, somewhat unkempt, with non-descript features and the characteristic lifeless eyes. He had approached Fr. John as he left the rectory to visit a homebound parishioner and addressed him by name. When the priest stopped, the boy grasped his right forearm, gazed into his eyes and projected a vision of two teenage boys in a classroom laughing while firing semi-automatic pistols at classmates at point blank range. Fr. John wrenched himself from the boy's grasp and the child fled. The boy looked exactly like one of the shooters in the vision. The priest called Argo immediately. When the call came, Argo was watching a breaking news flash of the massacre of thirteen students at a high school in the Midwest carried out by two eighth grade boys armed with semi-automatic pistols. The killing had stopped when the shooters turned the guns on themselves. Fr. John and Argo met to decipher what message Praggles was conveying by pointing to the tragic event.

Another week elapsed then both men received an email containing a link to a news story about the tragic death of a limousine driver in Las Vegas. The driver had suffered a heart attack while transporting four dermatologists from the airport to a seminar at a hotel on the strip. The physicians recognizing the symptoms of a coronary had called 911 to request emergency medical assistance. None of them knew how to administer CPR. By the time the EMT's arrived, the driver was dead. The need for Praggles to explain the thread running through these communications became even more evident as Argo and Fr. John puzzled over the meaning.

The next communication was mailed; both Argo and Fr. John received identical envelopes, each containing a copy of an article excerpted from a scholarly periodical. Neither a return address nor a note was included, but the fact that both men were recipients spoke for itself. The article described research based on Meta data showing a trend away from student activism occurring across elite campuses. The research presented statistical and anecdotal evidence that modern university students at the premier educational institutions saw financial success as the most important goal in their lives. The research pointed to a willingness to use any and all means to gain maximum leverage within the existing institutional structures. The purchase of ghost written essays for applications was rampant, as were many other forms of cheating. Unlike prior generations at the same universities, questioning the moral authority and methods of the established order was no longer part of the agenda. Several interviews with professors whose experience had bridged this span were included. They spoke of students focused on acquiring their ideas, but rarely challenging them. Each was troubled by the phenomenon, but none had an explanation.

This was followed a week later by a message delivered to each of them by the another minion. This one appeared to be a homeless woman; she had accosted each of them intrusively, made eye contact, and remarked that they should go see a particular, newly released science fiction movie. She had the characteristic empty eyes, and disappeared into the crowd immediately. Argo and Fr. John saw the movie together; it was a bloody, action packed thriller that portrayed a world where humanity was embedded in a made-up virtual world completely controlled by computers, robots and machines. The control was so seamless that all but a handful of people were unaware of the servile state of their existence.

When Argo and Fr. John discussed these diverse communications it was clear that only Praggles could tie the pieces together. Presumably the events were related. Was neurotic anxiety the basis for Praggles' suffering, or certain knowledge of coming catastrophe? Argo's experience was that Praggles possessed extraordinary powers of reasoning and observation, yet was also capable of errors in perception and judgment. Each new piece of the puzzle deepened the mystery. Another aspect of the communications that eluded their understanding was Praggles willing inclusion of Fr. John. Argo commented.

"Praggles is leading a cosmic scavenger hunt for us, and so far we are unable to process the clues. Something has to open up for this to make sense."

No Love Lost

IT WAS 8:30PM AND ARGO WAS EXPECTING Abdur, his young, Pakistani client at nine. His 8:00PM client had emailed saying a crisis at work would cause him to miss his appointment. Argo pulled Abdur's case notes and looked them over to focus himself. His friend Abigail, who administered Abdur's residency program, had left a message on his answering machine. She requested he discuss an altercation that had occurred between his client and the chief resident at the hospital, but the balance of the message was too garbled to decipher - so much for cell phones. Argo had met with the young doctor each week, and had been pleased by his willingness to engage in treatment. Abdur and his fiancé had used their sabbatical well. They resolved to continue with their plans to marry, and developed and were carrying out a clever strategy with their respective families. Argo marveled at their approach; they were going to let the two sets of parents choose to participate or not, but were also subtly steering them toward the choice they would prefer. Each had quietly informed their parents through a trusted intermediary of their intention to have a private civil marriage ceremony in one month, after which they would move in together and live as husband and wife. The emissary related this, and then confided to each set of parents that the couple had tried to arrange a traditional ceremony, but had been unable to find an Imam who would preside over a marriage not approved by the parents. He stated that although they were saddened by the scandalous rumors floating around the community, they loved each other so much that it was the only course left to them. The parents clearly had an opportunity to mend their relationship with their children, end the gossip in the community, and even to appear to be in control of the situation by taking over the marriage arrangements. There were indications that the parents of the two families had communicated with one another – a hopeful sign.

When Abdur arrived Argo could see from his expression that he was agitated; he waited for him to be seated.

“Abdur, you look like a man with something on his mind.” Argo began.

The response was hostile.

“Yes Dr. Masters I do, and am presenting myself to you for my scheduled mind control session so you can remove or at least suppress the unacceptable thoughts and actions that infect my heathen soul.”

Argo decided humor might dull the fangs of his client’s anger.

"I'd love to, but have left the battery, electrodes and rubber hose home today. If you tell me about your transgressions, I can decide which implements to bring to our next session."

Abdur's expressions morphed from anger, to puzzlement, to thoughtful, and then weariness.

"I apologize Doctor Masters; that was unfair. I do not really believe you would participate in such an effort. I am in trouble at the hospital again. One of the chief residents has asserted that I represent a danger to the patients and staff, and his claim is being reviewed by the administrator of the residency program."

Argo wished he'd been able to listen to Abigail's entire message.

"Why don't you tell me what you can about the situation."

Abdur attempted to speak calmly, but his gestures and the veins that appeared near his temples betrayed strong underlying emotions.

"Do you remember the news stories about a Muslim cleric name Sheik Ali Mohammed Rahman being arrested by the US Government for preaching jihad at a mosque in Brooklyn?"

Argo recollected reading of the arrest several months ago. The charges against him included claims that he had advised several of the terrorists who took part in the September 11th attacks.

"Isn't the government holding him at a detention facility while seeking to deport him back to Egypt for preaching terrorism?"

Abdur nodded.

"Yes, that's him. He was brought to our emergency room today after collapsing during a mandatory exercise walk at the prison. The security detail that brought him consisted of four plainclothes agents and four guards armed with automatic weapons. The chief resident who should have taken charge, instructed me to examine him; he claimed he was too busy. I asked the agents to remove the leg shackles and handcuffs. They were reluctant to do so, and I had to be very forceful to get them to acquiesce. They eventually removed the shackles and handcuffs, but then stood at the entrances to the examining room with their fire-arms ready as if an attack were imminent. All the other patients were scared. They gave me his medical file, and then ordered me to conduct all communications with the patient in English. They were very emphatic about it, and told me I could be arrested if I did not comply. It was a nightmare."

Argo had to manage his own feelings as Abdur spoke; his personal experience of the 9/11 attacks made it difficult to feel any sympathy for the old cleric. There was no amount of security precautions that he would have considered excessive for a prisoner like that, but he would not willingly allow his client to see his ambivalence.

"Were you able to examine him?"

"I was. I introduced myself and immediately the sheik attempted to speak to me in Farsi, he seemed to have guessed that I would understand. I told him we must speak English and asked if I might examine him. He agreed to be examined. He was dehydrated and his blood pressure was quite low. I took his medical history and concluded that his generally poor health and dehydration had caused his blood pressure to drop to a point where he lost consciousness. I gave him an IV drip to hydrate him, and told him to drink plenty of water. When he left, he blessed me, and I bowed my head in deference. The chief resident called me into one of the empty examining rooms. He was there with one of the staff doctors. He started shouting at me, and making accusations to the effect of me being aligned with murderous, evil, criminals."

Argo reflected back to Abdur.

"Big security details, high profile accused terrorists, and an abusive interaction with the chief resident. How did you respond?"

Abdur seemed surprised by the question.

"I felt his attack on the sheik was blatantly biased, and told him so. The sheik is a very holy man. He had been asked to examine the fatwas that had been declared by the Jihadists who were waging war against the United States. He declared that they were just. He did not do so because he is a murderous lunatic, but because he found them to be theologically sound. He is a highly respected and learned Muslim cleric, he has spent his life studying and interpreting the Quran. The chief resident relieved me of my duties and suspended me from the residency program, pending an investigation into concerns that my presence in the program could endanger patients and staff at the hospital. He said I was a potential 'lone wolf' terrorist!"

Argo's first hand recollections of the September 11th attacks on the World Trade Center were so visceral that he found himself unable to maintain therapeutic neutrality. He considered the sheik to be a thug masquerading as a holy man. Argo knew that if he failed to be authentic with his client, he could not provide effective treatment.

"Abdur, I must tell you something, and I'm not sure how. When you speak of this matter, I find myself overwhelmed by emotion. May I speak frankly to you about this?"

Abdur looked startled, then angry and defensive.

"Are you going to give me some moralistic mush about innocent victims?"

Argo waited a moment to let them both calm down.

"Will you hear me?"

Abdur shrugged.

"Do I have a choice?"

Argo averted his eyes. Direct and prolonged eye contact was considered aggressive in his client's community, and right now he suspected his eyes would communicate anger. That would not be helpful.

"Abdur, in my business we are trained to listen to our clients, and to recognize when we have an issue with what they are saying. Most of the time, clients are completely unaware when something they have said activates strong emotions, because we recognize and resolve the issues immediately. Occasionally, an issue is so powerful that we must share it with the client or risk losing the authenticity in our communication. In this case, I wish to communicate to you how I feel so that we are able to continue to speak honestly. I admire your direct approach to the issues you are dealing with, and particularly the courage you have shown in working with me - someone outside your community, in sticking to your resolve to marry, and for standing up for what you believe. We have established a good rapport, and I want to keep it that way. Are you with me so far?"

Abdur had been listening very intently, as if waiting for the other shoe to drop.

"Yes, I think so."

Argo knew it would be useless to approach the issue from a moral or political point of view; he would simply speak of his feelings in the matter.

"What I want you to know is that I was in the World Trade Center on September 11th. I saw things that were so horrible I would not describe them to you even if I could. There were almost fourteen hundred people trapped in the burning floors above where the first plane struck. As the floors became scorching hot and smoke filled, these people were left with the choice of burning and choking to death, or stepping out the windows. They were landing right in front of me. Human beings have many amazing abilities - empathy is one of them. Somehow, when I realized what I was witnessing, the experience of the choice each of those people had to make became present for me. The intervening years, the therapy, nothing has been able to help me deal with that. The Sheik was part of that attack, he supported it."

Argo saw Abdur's face flush.

"You do not understand..."

"Abdur, what is it that you will tell me that will make me understand? Can you imagine a situation where your best option is to jump out a window a hundred stories above the ground? Here is the bottom line, it is extremely difficult for me to participate in discussions of jihad at a logical level, my experience is too visceral. The soundest reasoning on earth will not take those images from me. I said 'Jihad' because, in this case, that is what motivated the attack, but feel free to plug in 'Crusade' or 'Cleansing' or any of the other vanilla words that murderous leaders use to enroll otherwise sane and humane people into slaughtering their fellow human beings. Huh? How the fuck will you explain it to me?"

Argo had never cursed while speaking with a client, and only then did he realize he had been shouting. He came around his desk and sat on the couch next to Abdur, half turning toward him. He could feel the tingling in his face, and knew it was red with embarrassment.

"I cannot believe I have gone off on you this way. I will understand if you feel my actions today are a deal breaker and you choose to end our work together. I wanted to make you aware of my feelings because the power of the work we do depends on our being able to communicate authentically. It was not my intention to lose control of myself and act abusively. I beg you to forgive me."

Abdur said nothing for a moment. His gaze seemed turned inward. When he spoke his tone was cold, calm and his manner polite.

"Dr. Masters, I suspect that my position on this matter occurs as completely barbaric to you, but you do not know what I know. I appreciate what you have done for me, and want to be certain you know that. I have been traversing unknown territory by speaking with you, and have been very relieved to find such a trust-worthy counselor; you have a benevolent and generous spirit. I am not certain what to do at this point, and would like some time to reflect on what is best before making a choice."

Argo knew that Abdur would not confront him with a choice to leave. If he chose not to continue, he would simply vanish. He was not sure whether this was a polite exit or a bona fide request for the space to make a choice. He raised his gaze to meet Abdur's briefly.

"Abdur, you are a doctor, and have dealt with enough patients to know that sometimes it is very important that they listen to you. Now is such a time for you. You are in an extremely vulnerable position. As your therapist and someone who cares about you, I am urging you to avoid making any major decisions until this can be sorted out. If you feel you must act, please call me first. If that is no longer comfortable for you, then please discuss your plans with your future wife. Will you promise me that?"

Abdur did not explicitly agree with Argo's request but told him he would think about what they had discussed, and get back to him with his decision in several days. Their session was over and Argo followed as Abdur exited to the waiting room, and strode toward the outer door. He turned as he opened it and said good night.

Argo was about to return to the office, when he saw Praggles gazing at him from a chair in the corner of the little room.

"Well, well Dr. Masters, your young doctor was very distressed at being denied access to his woman, but has no trouble defending indiscriminate slaughter. Do you have a diagnosis for that condition?"

End Game

ARGO SHUDDERED INWARDLY AT THE absolute zero of Praggles' presence. He walked to the door that led to the outer hallway of the building and locked it, then turned to his client.

"This seems to be my night for speaking to clients of my concerns, Abdur, and now you. I don't want to see you if I am not safe, and I will not. Will you promise not to harm me under any circumstances if we continue our work?"

Argo waited for the emotional projection he was certain his question would arouse, but there was none. Praggles looked somber.

"I will not harm you."

Argo opened the door to the office and waited for Praggles to enter and be seated. They sat and faced each other. Praggles began the conversation.

"My choice to work with you is unprecedented. Considering your observations and pondering the questions you asked, has resulted in clarity about events both current and past. I have existed since the beginning, yet never communicated my concerns to another being. I am intimately enmeshed in humanity's existence and see everything that takes place. From my vantage point I saw changes that were of concern to me. I came to you because of these concerns, but they were more than concerns. You were correct to say I was fearful. I had not recognized it as such, nor even acknowledged a capability to experience it. Now that I have seen these things, it is important to me to discuss this matter with you in its entirety. I will begin by telling you how I chose you."

Argo sensed a different energy from Praggles; calmer, almost sad. "Please do."

Praggles began: "It was apparent from the time of your birth that you were the recipient of grace from the Creator. Much spiritual activity and attention was devoted to you - there is no way you would know this, but it was very evident from my vantage point. Great care was taken to insure that you were healthy, safe and well nurtured. Sometimes this involved interventions on your behalf. Interventions of this nature are so subtly done, as to be invisible to human beings, and at their most obvious, appear to be graceful coincidences. You were given many extraordinary qualities, but common sense was not one of them. Left on your own, you would not have lived past childhood."

Argo was fascinated, and even a little embarrassed by what Praggles said. "Could you give me an example of one of these graceful coincidences?"

Praggles smiled indulgently.

"Certainly. When you were seven years old you lived by a bay. It was winter, the bay was frozen over, but the tide had broken the ice into large chunks. The ice chunks floated in the freezing water. You and your younger brother Franklin were having fun jumping from one ice chunk to the next and had gone out far from the beach. One misstep and you would both have drowned. Your mother, who thought you two were playing in the yard, suddenly had a premonition you were in danger. When she didn't find you in the yard, she ran to the beach. She spotted you and your brother on the ice, and waved to get your attention. Your mother knew you were in great danger, and calmly instructed you on how to return to the shore. The idea to look for you was not her own, but was put in her mind. She was very preoccupied at the time with your sick youngest sister. This is but one of a number of interventions on your behalf."

Argo remembered jumping on the ice flows with his brother; it was over forty years ago. They had lived in the big house on the bay in Northport. He had often marveled at how either of them had survived the foolish and risky things they did as children. Suddenly his mind made a connection with his experience with the rock in the road. Before he could mention it, Praggles began to laugh.

"I wondered how long it would take for you to ask about that. That occurred years later. At that time in your life, it appeared that you had turned your back on the Creator. You had even declared yourself to be an atheist. You often uttered blasphemy as if intentionally trying to offend the Creator you professed not to believe in, yet it still appeared that you were being protected. I placed the rock in the road to find out."

Argo was surprised by Praggles admission. "What if I had driven into it?"

Praggles reply was matter of fact. "You would have died instantly. The response to my blocking the road with the rock was immediate. There was no time to arrange for a graceful coincidence - you were told outright to stop the car. You did not attend to the first command because you were too surprised, but you stopped the car the second time you were commanded to do so. You are watched over to this day."

Argo was struggling to grasp having been a pawn in a cosmic struggle, and the next question burst from him. "Is that why you didn't kill me during our last session?"

Praggles' eyes narrowed reflectively. "No. Harming you was my reaction to the fear you revealed in me. I would like to tell you that I didn't kill you because I choose to follow the rules we agreed, however I continue to be puzzled by the fact that I did not."

There was an unasked question hanging in the air, both of them knew it. Argo could barely utter it. "Would it be accurate to say that you have interacted with me only as a means of communicating with the Creator?"

Argo was astonished at the change the question evoked in Praggles' demeanor. He sighed and his face reflected the stark emptiness of someone looking into the coffin of their last loved one. The arrogance was gone; his eyes assumed the look of someone gazing inward. "That is my hope. I have not communicated with the Creator since...the time of the fall, when I was cast out of the divine presence. I was created as the angel of light at the beginning, but became the angel of darkness. My role as the tempter began then. Over time it has become my belief that the creator intended for the rebellion to occur – even from the moment of my creation. What I cannot accept is the unbridgeable alienation."

Argo's mouth felt desert dry. Every instinct in his body, mind and spirit told him he was in way over his head, yet he was irrevocably inserted in the middle of an interaction of cosmic proportions. His biblical studies were replete with examples of ordinary people being called to participate in the divine unfolding. This was no time for second thoughts; he would keep putting one foot in front of the other. Praggles/Satan was the most un-recalcitrant, hard-assed transgressor and rebel in all of history; what could he now be seeing that would so completely cow him? Argo wasn't sure he was ready to find out.

"I have been intrigued by your messages during the two months since we last met. You have provided five communications during that time. Fr. John and I have gone over each of the messages but only you can show us the connection between them."

Praggles nodded. "Yes. The five events as well as the session with your client Abdur are six signposts to the destiny that is unfolding. I will elaborate."

My first message concerned the movement of nuclear warheads. Do you remember the incident I related to you of the five Afghani brothers being murdered in an attack by a military drone whose surveillance software had been programmed to produce false positives?"

Argo nodded.

"You will also remember that the programmer was a member of a group of hackers who compete with one another to manipulate strategically important computer software and systems."

Argo again nodded. "Yes."

Praggles continued. "The movement of the nuclear warheads described in the newspaper was accomplished by one of this group of hackers. He had been planning and working on it for years, and he executed it after announcing his intention to his compatriots. He was acclaimed among the group as having executed the most spectacular manipulation to date. Another member is about to upstage him. He has penetrated the Russian military computer networks and has managed not only to trans-ship a nuclear warhead, but to remove all traces of it from the military's inventory. This warhead is now stored in a private warehouse and is being offered for sale to the highest bidder. It appears that it will be sold to a jihadist who intends to transport it by ship to San Francisco and detonate it at midnight at the beginning of Ramadan. He fancies himself a Mahdi and wishes to bring about the apocalyptic prophesy of the sun rising in the West."

Argo felt a wave of nausea as the impact Praggles' story sank in. "That would be thousands of times as deadly as the September 11th attacks; the loss of life caused by such an event would be incalculable. Will this happen?"

Praggles shrugged. "Eventually. If not this time, then the next time or the time after that. Things have changed. It is now possible for a very small number of people to wield enormous power. Before we examine the details of any one thing, let me explain each of the signposts. Now let's consider the second message. Perhaps you will see the connection. What did you make of the massacre at the middle school in Ohio?"

Argo let his mind explore the two events. "If there is one message the two share, it seems to me that it would be "Life is cheap." The shooters took the lives of classmates then threw their own lives away. They seemed willing to trade whatever future they had for the opportunity to gain notoriety as the perpetrators of a massacre. What had the most value for them was the ephemeral fifteen minutes of fame."

Praggles nodded. "You have focused on the most significant aspect of the event. For a growing number of people, life has become so meaningless as to have little worth. I'm sure you have noticed that there is no shortage of suicide bombers?"

Argo nodded and Praggles continued. "The third message, the email containing the link to the news article concerning the four doctors and the dead limo driver illustrates the effects of the soulless direction you are heading in. The four physicians are typical of the profession; they are not healers in spite of the Hippocratic Oath they took. All their attention is devoted to a narrow band of medical knowledge the practice of which will bring them rich financial rewards. The term specialist seems to convey a senior level of knowledge, but it has been so long since most of them practiced general medicine, that they would be useless in most medical emergencies. They are emblematic of the consciousness of many modern professionals; they operate in a very narrow domain and are motivated primarily by acquiring prestige and accumulating wealth."

Argo decided to remain noncommittal until Praggles had explained his purpose for each of the messages.

"Okay, I can see that as a possibility. So tell me about the research article on the lack of originality in today's students."

Praggles proceeded: "It is part of the same story. The best and brightest of your society do not behave today as the best and brightest of any previous era. Having an impact on the world and its people has receded far into the background. The acquisition of power and wealth has become the primary motivator."

Argo was having difficulty getting his mind around this. "Why?"

Praggles responded immediately. "In a world where spiritual values are considered archaic, moral values dwindle. Eventually there are no absolute spiritual and moral values; everybody's voice carries equal weight. In that circumstance, everything becomes quantitative – mass is all that makes sense. These students are a product of an environment governed by that. It is possible to get into the finest schools based on quantitative scores on standardized tests. Moral character and service have been devalued as criteria. Good test scores; good finances and legacies are the primary means of access today. In my work it has become more and more difficult to test young people, especially if they are privileged. Morality has been reduced to a quantitative state - you are good if you get away with it."

Argo was tantalized by what Praggles was saying but he was not yet in possession of the key to understanding his client's perspective. "I can see that. But what about the movie? It seems to be saying something else. The movie depicted a world where humanity had been enslaved by the very machines they created. In the film the human race served the machines. What does that have to do with the loss of spiritual and moral values?"

Praggles stopped and peered at Argo for a moment. "I thought the message of the movie would be obvious to you Dr. Masters. You can't see it because you are looking at it backwards. The machines are not taking over humanity; they are what humanity has become. The technology humanity has immersed itself in promotes the profligate communication of the senseless to the farthest reaches of the globe without interruption. The very volume of the streams of meaningless data is like the weeds that choke the crop that would have fed your souls. Do you remember what I prophesized about the Tower of Babel?"

"Yes. That the Creator prevented mankind from completing the tower to save us from the self-destruction we would create otherwise."

Praggles raised his hands like a conductor leading an orchestra. "Yes. Now do you begin to see? Even the people who believe they are still living by spiritual and moral values have given themselves over to the influence of leaders who are merely celebrities in the media, but who are the antithesis of what they appear. Your Pakistani client believes himself to be a good and faithful servant of the Creator, and has no idea that the beliefs and values he has adopted are the manipulations of narcissistic, murderous, lunatics who delude themselves that they are holy men. You can find equivalents in all of the religions. Humanity is using all its science to squeeze out anything but its own voice, and that voice is leading it to fulfill an apocalyptic destiny. Given the path you are following, you can only go deeper into the wilderness. When billions of voices clamber to be heard, nothing can get through."

Argo was almost dizzy from the energy now emanating from Praggles. The flow of it had been building as he spoke and had now reached a point where he wondered if his hair was standing on end. He had to focus. Was Praggles saying that the end of the world was close at hand? Even if he was, Argo needed to help his client begin processing the information in a manner that allowed him some power to be with it. "If you believe this to be true, then the experience of fear would be a very logical and appropriate response. We have covered a lot of things and I want to be certain that I have understood you. Here is what I think you are saying..."

Praggles sat back and crossed his arms. He gazed at him intently as Argo began.

"More change has occurred in the human landscape in the last few centuries than in all preceding time. Much of this can be attributed to the application of advances made as a result of scientific, empirical inquiry. The fruits of this inquiry today can be seen in computer driven automation, virtual communications, high speed transportation, robotics, factory farming, weapons of mass destruction, and medicine, among other things. In and of themselves these accomplishments have transformed humanity and the planet, but there has been an unexpected dark side. Humanity has fallen in love with science and cast spirituality aside. It has resulted in an age where the acquisition and dispensing of human knowledge follows two trends.

The first is a de-emphasis of spiritual and philosophical knowledge and issues in favor of the technical and scientific. If a belief or phenomenon cannot be proven scientifically, it is considered primitive superstition.

The second trend is for people to specialize – to know a lot about a little. Doctors, engineers, lawyers, computer programmers, traders, soldiers and the like, all operate in finite domains of knowledge and activity. The result of jettisoning spirituality and the narrowing of individual knowledge is that human beings, as a rule, no longer look for the big picture, many no longer even realize there is a big picture. Increasing proportions of humanity never venture outside their tiny domains of expertise and relevance. This has led to a proliferation of products, services, and related activities that allow people to completely immerse themselves in busy little functions that completely occupy them. The term human being can no longer be applied to most of us; we have become 'human doings'.

Our addiction to science and technology has squeezed out the spiritual dimension. It seems that humanity cannot be its own guiding light, that without knowledge of the existence of a creator, the anchor provided by a transcendent truth, and a seeking of the divine will and wisdom that resides there, we are devolving into an increasingly myopic species. Our arrogance blocks an appreciation of the wonders of creation of which we are part and in which we are immersed, and paradoxically shields us from the enormity of our own ignorance. It is a popular belief today that creation has been driven by random evolution, and that we have essentially been placed here by chance. These beliefs have a cost. Eventually we will either literally destroy ourselves or simply eliminate all vestiges of the links to the Creator that allowed us to transcend our finiteness in the first place."

Praggles emotional projection output had leveled off then began to diminish as Argo had spoken. Argo knew understanding his client's torment somehow lessened it.

Praggles spoke.

"The only error in your assessment is the assumption that humanity has recently become even more blind - mankind has been stumbling around in the same circles for millennia. Your children are born with the possibility of becoming fully developed beings, but each of your various cultures quickly eviscerate any possibility of that by educating them in the collective folly handed down from generation to generation. What is different today from the past is the availability of unlimited communication. It gives the charismatic lunatics an edge; they can find each other and network their insanity.

It is impossible to say exactly how or when the prophesized end will occur, but I am seeing an exponential rise in activities that could contribute to that outcome. I 'fear' that it is coming."

Argo wondered if Praggles was ready to articulate his dread.

"The thing that puzzles me is why the destruction of humanity is so onerous to you – you will survive no matter what."

Praggles' answered without raising his voice, yet his words landed like a desolate shriek from the bottom of the pit:

"What is it that I and my minions will do then? What purpose will rouse us? You are all we have ever had, and when you are gone we will become meaningless and irrelevant for all eternity."

Argo and Praggles sat in silence. He guessed that the dread had subsided for him. The emotional energy Praggles projected had receded; replaced by a palpably bleak resignation. Argo was fascinated by the scathing language he'd used to assess humanity's accomplishments.

"You have a very low opinion of mankind's ability to reach solutions to its problems. Why is that?"

Praggles sneered.

"You would not understand the answer - you are as blind as the rest of them."

"Our agreement was that you would pay me by giving me knowledge. I want you to explain why you believe we are blind."

A look of contempt settled across Praggles' features.

"Your priest friend already tried to have that conversation with you, but you could not even hear what he was saying. Now you are asking me to explain the exact same thing."

Argo struggled to make sense of Praggles' statement. Was he referring to the conversation with Fr. John at the rectory after his second meeting with Praggles? If so - had he listened to all the conversations? Argo had to find out.

"Are you speaking about Fr. John telling me about meeting with an old monk from Tibet?"

"Don't try to be sly with me Dr. Masters - I invented sly. Of course I'm referring to that conversation. He was trying to explain that almost all of humanity, you included, is completely unaware of the makeup of your own nature, and thus have no ability to manage even your own behavior, let alone that of others. You were surprised by what happened with your client Catherine. He wasn't. You view yourself as dedicated to your clients, but are unaware of the strong influences that act upon you. You look for morality in books, because you don't know where you should look. By some cosmic coincidence you have allied yourself with a person who has objective knowledge of humanity's makeup and purpose. If you wish to know why you did not behave as you would have liked, or why Randall does what he does, or Abdur does what he does - speak to your friend the priest."

Argo was mystified by what Praggles said, but realized he'd digressed. There were much more critical issues here and the focus needed to be returned to Praggles.

"What is the next step?"

Praggles vexed look previewed his words.

"Next step?"

Argo knew what he was about to utter crossed a dangerous boundary, but his gut instinct was to proceed:

"I am puzzled that the idea of intervening to prevent the destruction of humanity is not something you have considered."

Praggles did not move a muscle for what seemed several minutes. He stared at Argo, but it was clear from the emptiness in his eyes that his thoughts were elsewhere. Finally he spoke.

"I do not think this state of affairs has come about by accident. If I act to alter them, it will be by making my presence known in an unmistakable manner. That would certainly shake things up wouldn't it? However, it would also create a confrontation with the Creator which would likely go poorly for me, and those under my dominion. Can you now understand my situation? It is through our conversations that it has become clear to me. Having gotten what I came for it is time to say goodbye."

Argo was overwhelmed. He felt unable to grasp the enormity of Praggles communication. He did not want the session to end here.

"You almost killed me during our last session. I don't know if you understand that my work with you has been motivated by a real desire to help you. We are at a juncture where I must say something to you that will be difficult for you to hear. I suspect you are right about the consequences of making your presence known to humanity, but we both know that is not the only choice available to you."

Praggles raised both hands palms forward towards Argo. The force of the gesture seemed physical - Argo felt slammed back in his chair.

"Stop! Do not say another word! Remain silent.

Yes, I realize that you have worked on my behalf, for whatever unfathomable purpose. Now you have some naïve idea that you will convince me to reconsider ancient decisions. That would be fatal arrogance on your part. Is that clear?"

Argo knew he was as good as dead if he continued. He raised his right hand, palm outward in a gesture of peace. He had nothing more to say.

Praggles peered at Argo for a moment, as if contemplating something, and then he was gone.

Argo was dazed, but knew it would be best to speak with the priest while it was all still fresh in his mind. He dialed Fr. John's cell phone; it rang three times before he answered.

"I just finished a session with Praggles. I'd like to debrief with you right now. Can you meet me at the Café Hercule at 57th and 8th in twenty minutes?"

Middle of the Mountain

ARGO DID NOT WANT HIS DISCUSSION with Fr. John to take place at his office; he couldn't get the idea out of his head that his client lingered there. The café where they met offered the strange privacy of the city; they were completely surrounded by other patrons, all busily chatting with their companions. In that convivial din, anything could be discussed without risk of being overheard or spied upon.

Argo went over every detail of the session. Fr. John listened and made occasional notes, but only spoke to prod him onward when he seemed stuck. Argo dumped his recollections; they would go back over it after he had gotten it all out.

When it was clear he was finished, Fr. John began questioning him.

"We had discussed the possibility that he was using you as a conduit, and he was. What he said about you being watched over...how did it make you feel?"

Argo shrugged.

"It allowed me to see that I have lived my whole life from an erroneous context; never considered that my actions made any difference, or were related to anything else. In fact, I spent years believing that nobody even cared that I was alive, especially my parents. I am trying to wrap my head around the idea that beings of cosmic significance have been aware of my life and woven it into their intentions."

Fr. John did not seem perplexed by this.

"The feeling of being on your own, unrelated to anybody and everything except those you chose to interact with is common today. One cannot live in our world and think otherwise. Everything seems to point in that direction, yet it is completely wrong."

The priest asked Argo to repeat the part of the conversation where Praggles had spoken of the gap between himself and the Creator as perhaps not unbridgeable. After Argo did so the priest whistled softly.

"What do you make of that?"

Argo's gaze was unfocused - he was looking inward.

"It jarred me. Who would ever have guessed that Satan would be wracked by existential angst relating to the projected destruction of humanity? I made the mistake of accepting his words at face value. Throughout the sessions I had the sense of witnessing something enormously significant - a turning point. In a typical therapeutic situation it would be routine to suggest that the client could initiate actions to alleviate their own issues; suggesting to Praggles that he intervene to alter the direction of human thought was intended to be exploratory. It terrified me to utter it, but it was the only thing I could see to focus him."

The priest's demeanor made it plain he was processing the events Argo related; at length he spoke.

"There was, in fact, no turning point. From the beginning there were two main obstacles to his seeking rapprochement. First was his unwillingness to admit he owed his existence to the Creator, and second he had too much pride to admit to those who followed him that he had been wrong."

Argo nodded, and the priest continued.

"After inferring that the gap might be bridgeable, he immediately contradicted himself. Clearly you were suggesting that he could do things to assist humanity in regaining spirituality. In the convoluted lie he has adopted to justify himself, that would be to reveal himself to humanity as God. He will offer himself as the supreme creator and seek to be worshipped. Let me ask you, what meaning did you attach to his statement about revealing himself to us being a provocation that will cause a conflict with the Creator?"

Argo pondered for a minute.

"I'm not sure; it sounds like an escalation of blasphemy. What are you thinking?"

The priest seemed to be having difficulty speaking, as if the words he were about to utter were better left unsaid.

"In your study of the bible, did you ever read the Book of Revelations?"

Argo nodded. "I did not study Revelations closely, but do recollect the Armageddon stories."

The priest went on.

"Some biblical scholars refer it to as the domain of madmen. Of all the books of the Bible, it made the least impression on me – until now. It is prophesy that deals with the events that are to take place at the end of the world - the last struggles between the Creator and Satan. The beginning of the end is a period where many who are influenced by Satan, falsely represent themselves as prophets or the Messiah. Then Satan and his horde emerge from the shadows to exert control overtly. Satan actively seeks the allegiance of humanity and succeeds in luring many to follow him. It is my opinion that Praggles was pointing to this."

Argo seemed troubled.

"What are you suggesting?"

Fr. John continued.

"His statement about your Muslim client being misled by murderous, charismatic lunatics in the clergy makes sense, especially if you look at it through the lens of Revelations. Today's media allows for some pretty strange characters to capture center stage. If you look at the tabloids and who gets elevated to prominence, it is clear that something alarming is occurring. What scripture so quaintly refers to as false prophets emerge and lead even the faithful down wrong paths. The Muslims take a beating for this, but you can find the same puffed-up charlatans in every religion. I am appalled by some of the fanatics embedded in the Catholic Church."

Argo nodded.

"Yes, but how do you separate the mystics from the fanatics?"

The priest answered without hesitation.

"In most cases it is not difficult to separate the two - 'By their fruits you shall know them' is a quote from the Bible's Book of Mathew. People who instruct others to commit murder, strap on suicide vests, and blow up mosques and churches full of people - duh! In other cases, where the evil is more deep seated, the same yardstick applies, but its application requires greater discernment. The truly evil are quite adept at concealing themselves; they act to block the good acts of those around them, and influence others to do their dirty work. But in the end, no matter how righteous a person claims to be, just watch their feet. If the direction their feet take do not match the words coming out of their mouth, then ignore the words and listen to their feet."

Argo smiled at the idea.

"That is a good way to put it."

The two sat in silence for a few moments, each trying to get their arms around what had occurred. Finally Argo broke the silence.

"What is there for us to do? You and I have been involved in this, and will continue to be in the future. I have no idea how to oppose a charismatic and satanic icon. We are good men, but how can we stand against such a being? Any thoughts?"

The priest drummed his fingers on the table as he considered Argo, clearly weighing what to say.

"If you are imagining this as a struggle between two icons, one good and the other evil, where people get to choose between the two, you do not grasp this. The vast majority of people on the planet, given the consciousness they now possess, lack the resources to appreciate such a choice. Even if they chose the 'right' icon, it would make no difference. They exist in a state of such scattered consciousness that they are useless - to heaven, hell and even to themselves."

The priest's statement scared Argo, but also jarred his memory.

"John, two times in my conversations with Praggles, once in the beginning and also this evening, he said something similar to that, and both times he mentioned you. He said that you and a very small group of others possessed the requisite consciousness that once was available to all people. It was such an odd statement, that it slipped out of my memory. What did he mean? It seems to me that the most vulnerable will be those who have no spiritual grounding or who have surrendered to formulaic beliefs. People with an authentic sense of wonder at the mysteries of creation and the divine will have the best chance of understanding what they encounter. I think..."

The priest placed a hand on Argo's shoulder to stop his exhausted colleagues rambling.

"Argo, my perspective on this is a bit more complex than I've been able to convey to you thus far. I am sure that it is no coincidence that you and I have been joined in this task. If you are willing, I will try to give you the beginning of an understanding of what I see now, but it will take time for you to truly understand. Do you have the energy and willingness to hear what I have to say?"

Argo was riveted to what the priest was saying.

"John, I will attend to every word, please give me a way to hold what we've witnessed."

Fr. John squared himself to the table and looked directly into Argo's eyes. Although he did not raise his voice, there was an emphasis in his words that reached beyond Argo's mind, penetrating both his feelings and physical body.

"Praggles observations, and the conclusions he has drawn are what they are, but he's very late to the party in terms of awareness. The sacred knowledge needed to live life properly would never survive in today's world. The drift of humanity away from that has been occurring for millennia. The velocity of that drift is now escalating but it has always been there. The wisdom is not lost, but has been hidden and preserved, first by an ancient brotherhood, and now by a brotherhood of initiates living in small communities in a number of locations around the globe. The knowledge to enable humanity to live properly and harmoniously does not exist within the Catholic Church, Orthodox Christian Church, the Jewish faith, the Muslim faith or the Hindu. Many of them had it briefly, but generation by generation, small modifications were made that eventually eviscerated the essence of the teachings. Evidence of its presence can be seen in each, but most of it is missing.

I was introduced to the brotherhood through the old monk I told you about. He became my teacher years ago."

The pieces were becoming clearer for Argo.

"You possess an understanding of things that goes beyond what I can logically account for. Even Praggles pointed to you as being someone who has a special understanding. You tried to tell me about it when we first worked together, but I wasn't really paying attention. I am paying attention now. What is it?"

The priest's face reflected the frankness of his voice.

"Argo, what you ask me to describe cannot simply be imparted in words. You will first sense it as a unique quality of presence in those possessing it. It must be sought; it cannot be given to those who do not seek it passionately. It can only be acquired by those willing to work long and hard to obtain it. It isn't about rote rules and dogma, or anything else that lends itself to a quick conceptualization."

Argo felt a surge of energy within that surprised him.

"John, I'm not sure why, but just hearing you speak of the possibility of acquiring this has been an awakening for me. If working with Praggles has given me anything it is a clear vision of the sleepwalk my existence is - I don't want to live like that any longer."

"Argo, if you are truly ready I will see to it that you have the opportunity.

I would prefer to be your teacher, but I must leave immediately. I must share what we have learned here with the abbot at the monastery of the brotherhood from which my teacher, the old monk, came. In the meantime, I am giving you the name of a friend to contact. Call him and tell him I sent you. He will introduce you to some of the tenets and practices that will help you prepare yourself. Do not mention the work we have been doing here to him unless you must."

Fr. John scribbled a name and phone number on the corner of the page in his notebook, then tore it off and gave it to Argo.

Argo was stunned that his ally was leaving.

"John, I don't know what to say - we both know there are more chapters to come in this tale. When are you leaving and how long will you be gone?"

The priest shrugged.

"I will leave as soon as I can make arrangements - probably in three or four days. The monastery is in an extremely remote place half a world away, and it is impossible to tell how long it will take to get there and back. There is no communication as we know it, but I'll try and get word to you from time to time."

Argo's mind was racing. What if Praggles returned while Fr. John wasn't available?

"Can't you send word through one of the other 'initiates'?"

A look of surprise came of the priest's face.

"Argo, you can handle this. I must go. The old monk who initiated me into the brotherhood gave me special instructions to return to the monastery and speak to the abbot if a certain event took place in my presence. I swore to him that I would do this. The event he spoke of occurred in your meeting with Praggles last night. Evidently, the brotherhood has been warned to look for this sign - God willing, they will be able to give us guidance."

Argo had no response. He would be on his own.

Neither Argo or the priest had paid attention to the time, both were surprised when a waiter brought the check and informed them the café was closing. They waited for change in silence. The two walked out together, and shook hands before parting. The priest gave Argo the cab that pulled up, and then started walking - lost in thought about what - God knows.